# FUGITIVE TRAIL

## ELIZABETH GODDARD

**LOVE INSPIRED** SUSPENSE
INSPIRATIONAL ROMANCE

**LOVE INSPIRED®SUSPENSE**

INSPIRATIONAL ROMANCE

ISBN-13: 978-1-335-72155-6

Recycling programs
for this product may
not exist in your area.

Fugitive Trail

This edition published by arrangement with Harlequin Books S.A.

For questions and comments about the quality of this book, please contact us at CustomerService@Harlequin.com.

Love Inspired
22 Adelaide St. West, 40th Floor
Toronto, Ontario M5H 4E3, Canada
www.Harlequin.com

**Printed in U.S.A.**

The God of my rock; in him will I trust: he is my shield,
and the horn of my salvation, my high tower, and
my refuge, my savior; thou savest me from violence.
*–2 Samuel* 22:3

Dedicated to all those who put themselves
in harm's way to protect us—both two-legged
and four-legged creatures.

## Acknowledgments:

Thank you to my new editor, Shana Asaro,
for asking me to write a K-9 mountain rescue story!
I've always loved these stories from LIS and this gave me
a chance to showcase my own dog (though not a K-9)—
an English mastiff named Solomon. As always, I so
appreciate the encouragement and support from my
writing friends—we've journeyed long and hard to get here!
All my gratitude to my agent, Steve Laube, for believing in
me. It goes without saying, but I'll say it anyway—
thank you, Dan, Christopher, Jonathan, Andrew and Rachel
for your patience with this novel-writing mom.

# ONE

*Southwest Rocky Mountains,*
*Colorado*

The wind picked up and whipped big snow-flakes around Deputy Sierra Young's head as she followed Samson, her K-9 mountain res-cue English mastiff, up the densely wooded incline. She maintained a steady pace but her heart rate increased along with her breathing.

She hoped the small plane hadn't crashed too high in the San Juan Mountains. That could make it impossible for her and Samson, as well as the SAR—search and rescue—volunteers, to reach the site before nightfall or the snowstorm grew worse. But they had to find the plane before they could rescue any-one.

Two snowmobilers had returned to the small tourist town of Crescent Springs, Col-orado, earlier this afternoon claiming they'd seen the prop plane go down but they hadn't been sure where it had crashed.

She'd brought Samson as far as she could before releasing him to find any human scent. Samson had been trained to find humans, whether air scenting for anyone in the wilderness or tracking a specific person. He was smart and used his skills to find whoever he was searching for. The other SAR volunteers searched downwind from Samson. It was important to spread as wide a net as possible. The victims could have escaped and gotten lost in the mountains, or they could be trapped in the plane. Or worse.

She couldn't think about *worse*.

*Lord, please let us find and save them, whoever they are.*

Before the weather turned too harsh or night took over. Sure, Samson could work through the night, but not in this weather. The terrain and elements during the winter months here in the Rockies were currently too harsh for searching at night. Sierra worked as a part-time deputy and K-9 mountain rescue handler for the county. She knew that Sheriff Locke would protect the volunteers, and if it became too dangerous to search, he would call it off.

Samson's massive two-hundred-pound

form plowed up the hill through the deepening snow, giving credence to his aptly picked name. Snow could tire out some breeds of search dogs and limit their time searching, but mastiffs were the stronger working-breed dogs, and Samson hadn't tired yet.

An old friend—Bryce Elliott—had given Samson to her when he was a puppy, and had even named him. After the attack when she'd been a detective in Boulder, she'd wanted a big dog, and Bryce had surprised her with the English mastiff. A pang of regret that she'd left her friend behind when she'd moved from Boulder stabbed her at the worst possible moment. She missed Bryce. But she needed to focus on this search.

The sheriff radioed he was calling the search, bringing her back to the present.

At the same moment, Samson alerted her.

"Wait, no. Sheriff," she said into her radio. "Samson…he's found something. Let me check it out."

"All right. I'm on my way to you."

Her leg muscles burned as she tried to keep up with the big dog scaling the incline until they topped it, then to a terraced ridge and a well-over-a-hundred-foot drop.

Sierra stood tall and caught her breath. Her heart lurched.

A red Cessna rested on the ledge—halfway on, halfway off. The banged-up plane looked partially crumpled on one side. She could make out a figure inside the cockpit, and another one outside, beside the plane. Both were utterly still.

Sierra radioed the sheriff. "I found it. I found the plane. I see two—" *Bodies*, but she didn't want to say the word. "We need to check and see if they're alive."

"Good work, Sierra," he said. "Wait there while I let everyone know to head your way. And…be careful."

"Always," she responded.

If the two people she spotted were still alive, it would be a difficult rescue at best, getting them down this mountain. The most difficult part would be saving the person inside that plane that teetered on the ledge. In the snow and cold, even if they had survived, hypothermia most likely would kill them if the SAR team didn't get here quickly and get them medical attention.

She signaled for Samson to remain then she hiked closer to the wreckage in the deepening snow. A man rested face down in the snow and would soon be completely buried. Sierra removed her glove and brushed the snow away then pressed a finger against his neck. His body was cold and he had no pulse. Sorrow bled through her.

She released a heavy sigh. SAR missions with Samson always started with the hope of rescue. Of finding a lost hiker or helping someone who'd fallen by bringing them to safety. Always the hope that she would find survivors and the day would end well. But more times than she'd like to admit, the searches ended in tragedy when they found victims of an adventure gone wrong.

The wind whipped around the mountain blasting the snow at an angle and causing a near whiteout. Not good.

She eyed the small plane and from here couldn't see the other person. Should she get closer and see if she could help?

She hoped the rest of the search team arrived soon. An eerie metallic sound resounded from the plane. Its position was precarious at best. Could the howling wind push it over? She spared a moment to wonder what these people had been thinking, taking the plane out on a day like today. The plane probably shouldn't have been flying in this weather, and she guessed that the weather had everything to do with the crash. But she wasn't here to question them; she was here to save them...if she could.

She crunched through the snow to get closer to the plane and look inside the cab.

The pilot remained inside, his body hunched over. It was possible that his position meant he'd remained warm enough, if he was still alive.

"Can you hear me? Are you all right?" She crept even closer to the plane.

The sheriff had said he and the others were coming. What was taking them so long?

The pilot shifted. Her heart jumped. She radioed. "Hurry, sheriff. The pilot is still alive. He's going to need medical attention…"

Metal scraped.

The plane shifted. Fear skated across her nerves. "The plane is in a precarious position. It could fall from the ledge at any moment. I'm not sure what to do!"

The radioed squawked but a burst of static meant she couldn't understand the sheriff. Panic built up in her chest. Sierra eyed the plane and the junk scattered around the crash site. She searched for anything she could use as a rope. Samson whined, sensing her growing anxiety.

"It's going to be all right, Samson. You found the crash site. We're going to save the man who's still alive." What was she saying?

She had no idea if she could actually save him, but she could hope. And she could try.

*God, please help me!*

Was there anything worse than finding someone and then being completely helpless to save them?

The man groaned inside the plane. She had to reassure him so he would hang on to the will to live.

"Hold on! Help is coming."

She peered at the wreckage. It would be too dangerous to try to get in and get him out with the plane shifting on the ledge. She had to find a rope.

The snow was quickly covering the scattered wreckage—duffel bag, sheets of metal, clothing articles. Then she spotted what she needed—a wire rope used in aviation.

She eyed the airplane then the top of the slope. Something must have held the SAR team up. She couldn't risk waiting if they weren't going to make it in time. She found a boulder on which to secure the rope and tied the other end around her waist. Then she edged slowly to the plane.

Sierra ducked under the broken wing. Nothing about this was safe. The plane was completely unstable, but that was the whole reason she needed to act—and act *now*. She had to get this guy out, even though, depending on his injuries, that could also be dangerous for him.

The mangled door creaked when she pulled it open and then toppled to the snow-covered ground. Sierra yelped and jumped out of the way. She could enter only on the passenger side because the other side of the plane was hanging near the ledge. She couldn't reach it.

"Help," the man called from inside.

Fear tried to seize her but she had to remain calm and focused, especially if she was going to have to do this alone. She leaned into the cockpit and inched onto the passenger seat to get a better look at the man. Blood covered his forehead and temple from a gash. It oozed from his lips. He likely had internal injuries.

"Can you hear me? If you can, give me your hand."

Maybe she could grab onto him and pull him out through this side of the plane. Medical personnel would go at this much differently, but there wasn't time to wait.

The man's eyes popped open. Those eyes. They peered at her and into her and through her. His face was almost unrecognizable under the blood and bruising but she had never forgotten those eyes.

Sierra froze. Damien Novack. Air whooshed from her. She couldn't breathe.

No. It couldn't be. "What… What are you doing here?" The question squeaked out of her making her sound feeble.

Afraid.

Somehow, even though he was injured and probably dying, he managed to offer her a sinister, bloody smile. To her horror, he lifted a weapon. Aimed it straight at her.

Screaming, she ducked as gunfire exploded then froze in place. Where was the sheriff? She glanced up hoping she'd see him coming over the ridge. Instead, she spotted footprints, barely visible as the relentless snow continued to bury them. The prints led away from the plane and tracked along the ridge until they disappeared completely.

Someone else had been on the plane.

Then she heard what sounded like the weapon tumbling from Damien's hand. She could hardly believe he had been able to shoot to begin with, given his obviously severe injuries. His anger and need to see her dead had been enough to drive him.

Heart pounding, Sierra peeked inside the cab again and Damien's eyes tracked her. "Doesn't matter that I missed. He's coming for you," he said.

"Who... Who is coming?" Dread filled her.

"You know who. He came for you before. This time he won't fail."

Raul Novack, Damien's brother.

Moments ago, she thought there couldn't be anything worse than losing someone she was trying to save. But now she realized that wasn't true. There *was* something worse. Indecision warred inside of her. She truly did not want to help this man. He'd perpetrated countless evils and if she helped him to survive, there could be more victims down the road.

But she couldn't serve as judge and jury. She couldn't take a life or refuse to give her best to save someone in danger—God would know, even if no one else did. She grabbed the weapon he'd tried to kill her with and set it aside.

Regardless of the fear that tried to strangle her, Sierra reached for him. "The plane is going to fall. Take my hand or you're going to die."

He coughed up more blood. "I'm as good as dead anyway."

Then his face went still. His eyes blank.

He was gone, and she knew it. He'd known he was going to die and he cared only about attacking her with his gun and his intimidating threats.

Samson barked. The plane shifted. Sierra reached for the man she knew to already be dead, but it was no use. She couldn't free him. The plane moved and she realized she had only seconds to escape.

She backed out of the open doorway and ducked just before the remaining broken edges of the wing could hit her. Still, metal scraped her body, eliciting a cry of pain, and snagging her coat. If she didn't get free, the plane would try to take her over the ledge too, causing serious injury when the wire rope wouldn't release her.

"I got you!" The sheriff appeared and slashed the arm of her coat away from her body and gripped her arms. "I got you," he said again, breathless.

She slumped to the ground, the adrenaline whooshing out of her body.

Samson licked her and whined, warming her frozen cheeks, and comforting the icy cold fear that had stabbed through her.

Damien Novack had been here. And he hadn't been alone.

She let her gaze follow the tracks and, in the distance, along the tree line, she noticed that a man stood watching. Damien's brother, Raul—

*He's coming for you...*

* * *

Bryce Elliott checked into his hotel across the street from the Crescent Springs Toy Store—the reason Sierra had given for returning to her hometown. Her father had been struggling to keep up with the store, and needed her help. Bryce had suspected health issues were involved too but Sierra hadn't said.

That wasn't the only thing she hadn't said. Bryce believed that her father was only part of the reason she'd given up her detective job with the Boulder police department. He suspected that Sierra had never gotten over the night Raul attacked her, even though she had been given the go ahead to return to work.

But no one else knew her as well as Bryce. She'd needed to escape Boulder, and maybe even escape Bryce. The place and the people served as reminders to her of what had happened. He was glad she had found a way to move on. Before she'd made that physical move from Boulder to Crescent Springs, though, she'd made an emotional move when she pushed him away. They'd been close and had been growing closer every day. He'd taken a risk with her, putting his heart on the line for the first time since being utterly rejected by Rebecca, a woman he thought he loved a couple of years before he met Sierra. But with Sierra, he'd been ready to try again. Then Raul and the night of violence happened. After that, everything between Bryce and Sierra had changed. He had sensed her slipping away from him, and had experienced the pain of rejection all over again.

He cared about her and was here for her, but that didn't mean he would let himself fall for her. Definitely not. None of what had happened between them should matter now.

What did matter now was that she was in danger, and Bryce wouldn't let her go through that alone.

He sucked up his nerve and crossed the recently plowed street in the throes of an ice festival, presumably the biggest event of the year for the small out-of-the-way town in southwest Colorado. Other than ice climbers, most people opted to visit Telluride and Purgatory in Durango to ski. Crescent Springs offered an ice park to celebrate the ice climbing sport—beginners and professionals from around the world came to the small town to climb the frozen waterfalls of the gorge.

Moisture surged on his palms as he drew near the toy store he'd seen only on the website before this moment. Bryce drew in a deep breath and pushed open the door. How would she react when she saw him? That question had kept him company as he traveled here from Boulder.

The smells of plastic and cinnamon and peppermint wafted over him. He had no idea if he would actually find Sierra here, amongst the toys, but it was a start. Aisles of toys blocked his view, but as he browsed, he noted the store was relatively crowded. An older man's voice offering customer assistance drew his attention to the cash register and counter at the back of the store. A young woman he didn't recognize stood next to the older man he assumed was Sierra's father. She took payment from the customer and bagged toys.

"Can I help you?"

The voice. *That* voice. Turning to Sierra, he grinned. In a flash he took in her bright blue irises, her lithe and petite form, and the perfect lips that often turned up in an amazing smile, but which now morphed into a huge O.

She gasped. "Bryce, what…what in the world are you doing here?"

"Ah. You're glad to see me." He instantly regretted his slightly sarcastic tone. "It's good to see you too."

A frown emerged on her face and seemed to war with a tenuous grin.

"Well of course. I mean…of course I'm glad to see you. Why wouldn't I be glad to see you?" She reached forward and hugged him. This was the Sierra he loved—well, loved to see. She was wonderful. Except he sensed her wariness.

When she released him and stepped back, he saw the fear flashing in her eyes. Her face shifted as though she was searching for the right response, though he saw a spark of amusement when she noted the section of the store he'd stopped in. "Any particular type of baby doll you're looking for? I'm guessing this is for a niece? Or do you have…um…a daughter?" Sierra handed him a doll.

Like a fool he took it automatically.

"No. I don't have a daughter." It had been only a year since Sierra had left Boulder, and they hadn't kept in touch. "I'm not married and don't suddenly have a young daughter." He put the doll back on the shelf. "Nor do I have a niece."

He jammed his hand into his pockets, wishing he could go ahead and shrug out of his coat. It had kept him warm outside, but in here he was downright hot.

Sierra turned and walked away, still lacking the usual bounce in her step that he hadn't seen since she'd been attacked in Boulder.

"You still haven't told me what you're doing here," she called over her shoulder. Then she stopped at the counter. "Are you here for the ice climbing festival? I didn't know you were a fan. You might have said something back when I was in Boulder—we could have visited my hometown together." Sure they could have visited her hometown together while they were still "together." A pain flitted across her features. Had she forgotten that in Boulder, after Raul's attack, she'd distanced herself from him? No. And that made his appearance all the more awkward.

He stared too long, struggling to find the words. "I came to check on you."

A deep bark resounded from somewhere inside the building and rattled through him. "And Samson. I…missed him." *And you, Sierra.*

*I'm worried about you.* But he kept that to himself for now.

She eyed him, then walked around behind the counter. The man he'd seen earlier stepped from the back room. "Dad, this is Bryce Elliot. I used to work with him in Boulder. Bryce, this is my dad."

"Nice to meet you, Mr. Young."

"Call me John. It's nice to meet you too.

My daughter told me about you. You had her back when she was there in the city. Thanks for taking care of her for me. You can stick around if you like and keep up the good work." John winked at Bryce then grinned at Sierra.

She gently elbowed her dad and scowled at him, though love poured from her expression. "Dad. I'm perfectly capable of taking care of myself."

"And me. Your daughter took care of me too," Bryce said. They had, in fact, saved each other from certain death. He had no idea how much Sierra had shared with her father about what really happened. Bryce suspected she would have kept most of it from John, choosing to spare him the pain of knowing what his daughter had gone through.

"You want to see Samson?" she asked.

"You know I do."

"Come on back." She led him through the door past an employee area where boxes of toys were waiting to be stocked. Then through another door into a kitchen where Samson popped up to greet them. "We have an apartment at the back of the store. It takes up two floors. It's enough for the three of us. Me, Dad and Samson." She rubbed Samson's head.

Wagging his tail, he barked and lumbered over to Bryce. "Wow, he's gained some more weight."

"It takes about three years for them to be full grown, and he's about four now. He could still get bigger, but I train him often and keep him in good shape."

"I'd say that I named him appropriately."

"Well, I kind of liked your initial suggestion of 'Tiny' for a name, but I think you're right. Samson suits him."

Bryce leaned toward Samson and ran his hands around the dog's ear and enormous head. "Hey, buddy. How're you doing? Did you miss me?"

He received a wad of drool across his face and shirt. Bryce smiled to hide his inward cringe.

"You're the one who got him for me." Sierra's tone told him she was thinking about the reasons why.

"You said you wanted something big." He pet Samson, then glanced up.

She crossed her arms and gave him a pointed look. "Why are you really here, Bryce?"

His stomach sank as he noticed something in her eyes. "You already know."

"You're here because Raul and Damien escaped prison."

He nodded. Should he tell her that his thoughts went immediately to her when he heard the news? "I wanted to make sure you were okay. Did Captain Stephens call you?"

"I called *him*." She gestured for Bryce to have a seat at the kitchen table. She grabbed mugs and poured coffee without asking. Sugar and nondairy creamer were already on the table.

"Why did you call him?"

Sierra took a seat and then placed her elbows on the table. She pressed her face into her hands. "A plane crashed yesterday."

"Oh, no."

"Samson and I found the crash site. The state is working to recover the bodies. One died before I arrived. One survived only minutes after I reached the plane. But before he died—" horror crept into her eyes "—Damien tried to kill me. He shot at me. I dodged that attempt, but then...then he told me that Raul was coming for me."

"Oh, Sierra... I don't know what to say." He'd heard about the escaped convicts on the news like everyone else in Boulder and immediately contacted his old boss and BPD captain for the details.

"That's not all." Her voice cracked and, though she tried to appear unaffected, he didn't miss the shudder that ran over her. "I saw footprints in the snow from a third person—someone who escaped the plane alive. Then I saw him, Bryce. I saw Raul. He was on the edge of the tree line. He just stood there watching. If the sheriff and SAR team hadn't caught up to me, I don't know if Raul would have come back to the plane and tried to kill me."

She rubbed her arms and stared out the window to the woods. "As soon as I saw him, I tried to point him out to the sheriff, but Raul had disappeared. It was snowing hard so you could barely see anything. I wanted to go after him, but the sheriff wouldn't let me. If the sheriff hadn't seen the tracks in the snow before they were buried, I'm not sure he would have believed me about the presence of another man—and I'm still not sure he believes it was Raul."

"Why not?"

"He might have thought I was seeing things. I failed to hide how shaken I was at seeing Damien."

"What did the sheriff do? I hope he took action."

"He sent a couple of deputies to search

the area, but the storm and nightfall forced them to return before they found anything. They did retrieve the body of the unidentified deceased man though. My understanding is that a team will try to retrieve Damien's body today. I hear they suspect the other man worked for the brothers on the outside and helped with their prison escape. I guess Raul and Damien escaped prison and thought they'd get revenge before they disappeared forever. But Raul… He's out there somewhere, Bryce."

And Sierra was terrified. She wouldn't say the words, but Bryce could see the truth she tried hard to hide. She was tough and trained to protect others as well as herself, but anytime you became a target, even as a member of law enforcement, there was nothing wrong with a little healthy fear.

It was all Bryce could do to remain in his seat and not rush to her. Take her in his arms. He'd missed her since she'd walked out of his life. He'd been such a fool to let her so easily slip away.

"Sierra. I'm so sorry."

"You didn't have to come all this way to tell me that," she said. "You could have called."

He continued to pet Samson, rubbing his neck and behind his ears. "I don't have your number anymore." She'd changed her number—and she hadn't given him the new one. And besides, he'd wanted to do much more than say he was sorry.

"Fair enough, but you knew where to find me. You could have called the toy store."

Bryce cleared his throat. "I *did* call." And left a message that it was important and to please call him back.

"Oh. Okay. I didn't get that message. It's just Dad, me and Jane, our part-time help, working the store. Whoever took the call must have forgotten." She shrugged.

When she'd first seen him, she'd hugged him as if glad to see an old friend—glad and yet edgy. Now she seemed downright irritated, like she didn't want him here at all. He partly understood. He was a reminder about what happened. But then, Samson served as a daily reminder too, since the dog's sole reason for being in her life was a result of the attack in Boulder.

As a detective with the Boulder Police Department, Sierra had been instrumental in putting notorious killer Damien Novack in prison. Damien had headed up an arms and drug trafficking organization and had committed numerous heinous crimes and murders. After Damien's conviction, his brother,

Raul, had come to extact revenge on Sierra, and attacked her in her home. Bryce had barely made it in time to save her. Raul had tried to kill him as well, but Sierra had saved him too.

Bryce wasn't sure either of them had ever quite gotten over that violent night.

"Doesn't matter." He could shrug too. "I'm here now."

"And so you are." She arched a brow again.

He resisted the need to shift away from her piercing gaze. Was he prepared to stay even if she didn't want his help? He wasn't entirely sure how to take her reaction to his presence, but the fear in her blue eyes over the news of Raul remained.

And Bryce knew then that he would remain too—until the threat on her life was eliminated.

# TWO

Sierra rose from the table and moved to dump her drink so she could hide her trembling hands. She was still working to get over what had happened yesterday—the image of Damien's dark eyes and his intimidating words still fresh in her mind. Yesterday's experience would have been traumatic even if the man hadn't been an escaped prisoner who had come for her. Trying to save a man and watching him die like that had felt like a fist squeezing her heart tighter and tighter, crushing her.

And then to see Raul watching her from the trees…

As if that wasn't enough, Bryce apparently thought he could walk back into her world and she would welcome him to save her again—as if he was her knight in shining armor? On the one hand, that he would do such a thing warmed her through and through. But on the other hand, she didn't want to feel that way about his sudden appearance. They'd been through enough already.

Before Bryce, she'd cared deeply about someone on the Colorado State Patrol, but he'd been killed after he'd pulled a speeding driver over on the highway. His death had been senseless. It had been hard for her to get over it, but time had eased the pain enough for her to be ready to try. She had been close to letting Bryce in when Raul's attack came. He'd almost died.

Sierra wouldn't let herself care deeply or love someone in law enforcement again. There was too much pain to be had, something she knew from experience.

She sighed heavily. She truly had no idea how she really felt about Bryce's appearance. The moment she'd seen him in the aisle next to the baby dolls, her heart had stumbled, then begun to beat erratically until she'd calmed herself and reminded herself why she had to guard against caring too much. But that had always been hard for her when it came to Bryce. His sturdy form, strong jaw and huge dimples when he smiled had always made her heart jump around, but adding to that, he could be tough as steel one moment, then instantly turn gentle and sensitive and caring the next. She was surprised someone hadn't snagged and married him already.

"Listen." He remained at the table, toying with his mug. Samson lay at his feet, taking up half the space of the nook.

It was a picturesque moment, one she wouldn't easily forget.

"I know my sudden appearance today is a surprise to you. But I couldn't stay away. Not when I heard about Raul and Damien."

That news hadn't filtered all the way to the small town of Crescent Springs—not until they'd found the crashed plane. That Bryce still thought of her, and that some part of him had remained committed to her, could melt the cold places in her heart. And that wasn't a good thing. She'd tried to forget him and now he was here.

She'd hurt him before. She'd hurt the both of them. Could she really turn around, face him and ask him to leave? Washing the mug off, she tried to figure out what to say.

She continued to rinse the few remaining dishes in the sink. "So, what are you going to do?" she asked.

"I'm staying in town for a few days." His chair scraped the floor as he scooted it away from the table.

Oh. Okay. Hmm.

Facing him, she crossed her arms and leaned against the counter. "Don't you have a job? Did you take vacation or something?"

"I'm taking a few days off." He studied her as if waiting for her reaction. She kept her emotions hidden away.

Bryce turned his attention to the dog. Samson was a great distraction when one was needed. She totally got that.

"Is it always this crowded in town?" he asked. "Or is that just because of the ice festival?"

"No, it's not usually so crowded. The town becomes an ice climbing mecca during the festival." The timing of the prison break couldn't have been worse. The tourists and fans that flooded the town—so many strangers here—could make it easier for Raul to hide in the chaos and get to her.

If only…

Bryce glanced up at her. Not even the hint of a smile curved his lips. And why should there be? There was nothing to smile about under these circumstances. Bryce showing up because of the Novack brothers only served to emphasize the way the horrors of the past were coming back to threaten her again. Maybe even threaten Bryce again too. Still, the look in his eyes—He wanted to know how she felt about him being here—of course, he would want to know. But she wasn't sure herself.

"You know." She smiled. "I have this amazing guard dog, compliments of you. Samson wasn't there before, when the attack happened. But he's here now so you didn't need to come for me."

A pained look skittered across Bryce's face. Had she imagined it? At the sound of his name, Samson lifted his head. Bryce ran his hands through the dog's fur. "And I missed Samson, okay? I needed to come see my buddy and make sure you were treating him right."

Bryce's grin ignited memories in her. She'd adored his grin before. She couldn't let herself adore that grin again.

"I appreciate you coming to check on me, Bryce. Really. But there's no need to worry about me. I'm fine—and I'm sure Raul will be captured soon."

He crouched to get a better angle to rub Samson's enormous belly. The dog was really too big for this kitchen.

"Yeah. Maybe. In the meantime, why don't we have dinner tonight? You can tell me about life back here in Crescent Springs."

Dinner. Two friends catching up. Not a date. As long as they were both clear on that point. "And you can share what you've been up to. Catch me up on the Boulder PD." Wistfulness washed through her. While she loved working here and being close to her father, there were aspects she missed about the daily grind of detective work in Boulder.

Bryce stood to his full height, his silver-blue eyes taking her in. An old, familiar stirring hit her, and she realized how much she'd missed this man. She'd always felt drawn to him. But then, that was why she'd been deliberate about putting emotional distance between them.

"I don't have any inside scoops for you. I don't know what's going on with BPD."

She glanced at him. That didn't sound good. "Why don't you know what's going on?"

"I'm not working with BPD anymore."

Okay. That surprised her. "Why didn't you tell me?"

"I'm telling you now." He winked. "I've been a private investigator for a year now. That and working security."

She nodded, taking it in. "That had always been your dream." She remembered that much. "Good for you, Bryce. I'm glad."

Bryce held her gaze captive for a few breaths longer than necessary. There was so much more she could say to him.

He approached her and, in two easy steps, he stood much too close. Samson, who had stuck by Bryce's side, decided to wag his dinosaur tail and it thumped against her leg.

"Just so you know, I'm here until Raul is back in prison. I'm here for as long as it takes."

Sierra stared into his eyes. If only she could send him away. It would be safer for her heart. But his proclamation had the strange and unbidden effect of reassuring her that she would be safe as long as he was here. Between Samson and Bryce, no one would get to Sierra. And maybe it was okay to accept his help. After all, it had been only yesterday when she'd looked into Damien's vengeance-filled eyes right before he died. Only yesterday she'd seen Raul watching her.

Bryce suddenly took her hand. "Breathe, Sierra. It's going to be okay."

She hadn't been breathing? She slowly drew in air along with the hint of his musky cologne. "Is it? You didn't see what I saw." She hadn't meant to show him how scared she was. She didn't want to be scared. But this situation made her anxiety impossible to ignore. "You didn't see the hate in his eyes. He wasn't even afraid of the fact that he was about to die. All he cared about was getting to me. His last words were nothing more than evil. His brother is no different than him, and Raul succeeded in getting to me before."

And both she and Bryce had almost died.

A shudder rolled through her.

She tried to hide it but Bryce didn't miss the effect Damien's words had on her. Without a second thought he wrapped his arms around her. As a friend. Nothing more. Someone who cared for her deeply—and platonically.

"It's going to be okay. I hope some part of you knew that I would come. We've been through so much together. We faced off against Raul before. If he comes for you, we'll face him again and win—together, Sierra. That's why I'm here. To face him with you if it comes to that."

Though uncertainty about his decision to come had plagued him, now Bryce was more than glad he'd decided to head to Crescent Springs. Whether she had realized that she needed him before, he didn't know. But the way she held on to him now told him she would accept his presence, at least for the time being.

He eased away and gripped her arms. "I'm here for you."

In her eyes he could see that she didn't

*want* to need him. He took a step back even as she did too. "See you at dinner?" he asked.

She nodded. "Okay. Sure."

"How about the Crescent Springs Café just across the street." That should be easy.

"It's going to be crowded." She shrugged. "We could eat here."

"We could. But then your father would hear our conversation."

She nodded. "Right. I don't necessarily want him to know all the danger I've had to face or am facing now. I haven't even told him the worst part about yesterday." She rubbed her arms. "I need him to know. He needs to be safe and remain cautious, but I know how much it will hurt him to learn all the details of what I went through before, and that it followed me here."

"I'll be praying for you," he said.

Her eyes widened. "Looks like you have a lot to share with me, then."

Right. He'd found God. Or rather God had found him since Sierra had left Boulder.

"So the café it is."

She smiled. "I'll call and let them know to save us a table. I'm friends with Miguel, the owner."

"Sounds good." He left her standing in the kitchen petting the gentle giant he'd given her four years ago. She'd remained in Boulder for three years. When Samson had been old enough she'd trained him for K-9 work. Just before Samson had become an official part of BPD, Sierra had moved to Crescent Springs. Bryce got the feeling that the timing wasn't a coincidence. Sierra hadn't wanted to put Samson in harm's way or lethal situations.

He headed out through the toy store and gave a small wave to her father and the young woman Bryce assumed was Jane. She didn't look a day over twenty. As he exited the toy store, he realized the anticipation he felt about tonight's dinner with Sierra felt so much like a date when it shouldn't. She'd hurt him before, and he knew Sierra well enough…she would hurt him again if given the chance. Regardless, Bryce was only here to keep her safe. Sierra was in danger. That he found himself wrapped up in protecting her against a Novack brother again seemed surreal. But he would see it through until the end.

If only he could shake the feeling that it wouldn't end well. They had survived the last time. Could they survive this time?

He hesitated before crossing the street and leaving the toy store. But he reassured himself that while Sierra was at the toy store and surrounded by people, she should be safe. He walked the growing crowds to see if he spotted any familiar or unwanted faces and called his old boss from the Boulder PD on his cell.

"Bryce." The man was breathless. Traffic resounded in the background. "Good to hear from you. Since the Novack brothers' escape, we've been trying to find out everything we can. Where are you?"

*Three steps ahead of you.* Bryce leaned against a storefront and watched the toy store across the street while he talked. "Crescent Springs, Colorado."

"Oh, you're staying close to Sierra then. You obviously know about the plane crash."

"Yes. And I'm here with her until this is over."

"Don't forget that you sent them to the penitentiary too. You could be in as much danger."

"I'm well aware of that, don't worry. But I don't think that I was their primary target since they headed straight for Crescent Springs."

"But now that you're there, it's easier for Raul to get at both of you. That said, I don't blame you for being concerned about her." A car door opened and shut. "You're a good man to make sure she's all right. I'll stay in close communication with Sheriff Locke there in

Crescent Springs as the state and NTSB work through this so we're all on the same page. I don't need to tell you to watch Sierra's back, but please watch your own."

"I will, don't worry. I'm sure someone will spot Raul soon. He couldn't have lasted long in the elements so my guess is that he would have made the closest town."

"Crescent Springs."

"Which is hopping right now for a local ice festival. If he's hanging around, someone's going to see him."

"On the other hand," his old boss said, "he's smart enough to know that, with the plane crash, we're onto him. He might get as far away as he can rather than trying to get to Sierra."

"Whatever the case, let's hope he doesn't get to Sierra." The state was searching and local law had been called in, as well. Sierra wasn't out there searching for the criminal for obvious reasons. Bryce was glad that Sheriff Locke hadn't involved her.

"I'm with you. And Bryce? It's good to be working with you again. I wish you would have stayed with the BPD. You're always welcome to come back. We could always use another good detective."

"Thanks for the vote of confidence, Captain. I'll keep that in mind." At the very *back* of his mind. He ended the call.

Bryce leaned against the wall to watch the tourists entering the shops or merely window shopping.

Across the street, next to the toy store, he spotted a big man, his hood covering his face. The guy's build was the right size. He could be Raul.

Sierra appeared in the glass doorway of the store, stepped out onto the sidewalk and turned left to walk up the street. Where was she going?

His gut tensed. Bryce started across the street. The big man turned and walked away from the store as if to follow Sierra.

Bryce trailed him, picking up his pace. If this was Raul gunning for her, Bryce couldn't let him hurt Sierra. Nor could he let him get away.

The man increased his pace and headed directly for Sierra.

"Sierra! Watch out!" Bryce shouted but he wasn't sure if she could hear him over the bustling crowd and the traffic.

Sierra jerked around at the same moment the man was on her. He grabbed her, then threw her against the wall. He wielded a knife, but Sierra dodged his strike.

"Hey!" Bryce called out as he weaved through pedestrians and sprinted toward Sierra and her attacker.

The man jerked his attention to Bryce then threw Sierra down hard as if she was nothing but a rag doll. He pushed his way through the tourists to escape, bumping shoulders with people as he passed, and knocking a man and his child over.

Bryce caught up to Sierra and tried to help her to her feet.

"Go, get him!" She pointed. "I'll radio the sheriff."

Bryce ran after the man, but the attacker climbed onto a motorcycle and sped away. The chase wasn't over yet though. The traffic and tourists would slow the motorcycle and that would be Bryce's only chance of catching him. Bryce pushed himself, dashing between cars and people, shouting that he was coming through. The motorcycle turned right at the corner, away from the heavy traffic in the town's center. When Bryce made it to the corner, his legs slowed. He was good for a marathon but not for a sprint. Up ahead, he spotted the motorcycle speeding out of town.

There was only one main highway out of town, but there were numerous forest service roads. Bryce would never catch up to the man he suspected had to be Raul, but once noti-fied, the Colorado State Patrol would ramp up their search. Bryce wanted to believe that Raul would be captured. The fact that the convict had stayed around the area this long knowing that law enforcement was search-ing for him didn't reassure Bryce about Si-erra's safety.

Catching his breath, Bryce turned to make his way back to Sierra.

What would have happened if Bryce hadn't been there, watching the toy store when she was attacked? Would Raul have gotten the best of her despite her defensive efforts?

He couldn't bear it if something happened to her. Bryce would camp out at her place if that's what protecting her required. He had the feeling the hotel across the street might not be close enough.

# THREE

That night Bryce had dinner with Sierra as planned, in spite of the events of the afternoon. In spite of Raul's attack on her in broad daylight. The guy had no fear.

That alone had shaken Bryce to his core, though he tried to hide that fact from Sierra. He'd also tried to dissuade her from dinner at the café.

"I won't let him ruin my life here," she'd said.

After chasing after Raul and failing to capture him, Bryce had found Sierra in her kitchen, calming her nerves by petting Samson.

And now here they sat across from each other in a booth, trying to pretend everything was normal. Trying, and failing.

He'd been relieved when the waiter took their barely eaten food away. Neither of them had much of an appetite, and in that way, Raul was succeeding in ruining her life, as she put it.

Add to that, here in the café, they were probably too exposed.

"I'll see you back home," he said. Maybe if he stuck close to her Raul wouldn't be so bold. And maybe law enforcement had chased him far from here after today. In the meantime, he'd seen an increase in state law enforcement in town, adding to the county sheriff's meager presence. Sierra was as well protected as she could be.

But until he heard that the criminal had been caught, he would remain on high alert.

Nodding her agreement, she eased from the booth. "I'll need to take Samson for a walk. Want to come?"

"Of course. I wouldn't mind spending more time with him." He hitched a grin. "Oh, okay, and you too."

He kept the conversation light, but neither of them was feeling it. The heaviness of Raul's escape and pursuit of Sierra was pulling them both down.

"You know, walking Samson could be a problem if Raul is still here in town." Walking a dog was one of those daily routines that tended to follow a predictable pattern—and that could be dangerous, even if the dog was a massive K-9 mountain search dog.

"It's not like it can be helped." Her eyes

glistened in the low lighting of the café. "Samson has to be walked."

"Maybe I can do that for you instead."

She shook her head. "I won't put you in danger like that."

He knew, like him, she hoped it would be over soon.

Sierra paused at the door to thank Miguel, the café owner. The man's smile and warm gaze told Bryce that he was interested in Sierra. Bryce swallowed the shard of jealousy that surged up his throat. Then he escorted her across the street and through the store. Samson's deep throaty bark could be heard through the walls.

"It's easier to go through the store than to walk all the way around the building and storefronts, through the alley and then back around, especially when the snow can get too deep and isn't always plowed or shoveled. It's a weird setup, I know. But living at the back of the store is super convenient for Dad."

In the living room, her father sat in a recliner and flicked through television programs.

Bryce peered through the blinds at the dark woods. The light coming from the windows chased away few shadows. "It's convenient, true, but it certainly isn't the best setup for your current situation."

Sierra grabbed the leash off the hook. "Good thing I've got my K-9 and my handgun."

Right. Good thing. "Better keep the gun with you at all times then." She certainly hadn't had it with her today.

She nodded, but didn't acknowledge his comment any further, turning to her father instead. "How was dinner?" she asked. To Bryce, she said, "He insisted on warming up leftovers—fried chicken tenders and green beans—in the microwave."

"Probably better than what you ate at that restaurant." Her father chuckled.

"Right. My cooking isn't the best, I know, Dad. But the café's food is definitely better." Sierra attached the leash to Samson's collar— more a formality than an actual restraint, due to Samson's size.

She started to open the back door. Bryce touched her arm and leaned in to whisper. "I think it's a good idea to avoid going out this back way for the foreseeable future." He wouldn't say more in front of Sierra's father. He wasn't sure how much she had shared with the man.

She frowned and nodded. "What was I thinking? You're right."

She led Bryce and Samson back through the storefront. She unlocked and then once again locked the door. Anxiety settled in his stomach. He shoved through the deepening snow and a snow berm to get to the plowed street. "I'll be here first thing in the morning to shovel this away so customers can get to you."

"It's a problem, to be sure."

Snowflakes coated them both but being with Sierra seemed to add warmth to Bryce's layers, despite the cold dread that coursed through him.

As they walked, keeping to the freshly plowed street as opposed to the un-shoveled sidewalk, he didn't want to break the silence but he needed to say the words. "Samson is a deterrent, but be cautious even when you're out walking him. His protection isn't foolproof."

"And yours is?" She arched her brow again.

He almost smiled at that—he'd missed seeing her feistiness on a regular basis.

"You know what I mean," he said. Someone bent on harming her could shoot Samson and then Sierra too.

"I didn't thank you for today. You distracted Raul, pulling his attention from me and then he ran from you. Not me. *You*. If you hadn't been there maybe I could have won the fight, but I can't be sure. Just like before, you were there in time, Bryce. I owe you. But today drove home that you're putting yourself in danger by being here." Sierra turned to him, her breath puffing out white clouds. Snowflakes clung to her lashes.

"Don't tell me that you're worried about me?" Okay, that was just plain wrong—it sounded like he was asking her to say how much he meant to her. He wasn't going to flirt with her.

Sierra didn't answer.

That's because she probably knew he didn't want to know the real answer. Either way. He ignored the painful memories of their past and his attraction to her. Samson's low growl drew his attention to the animal and then the woods just beyond the line of buildings. He had suspected those woods were going to be a problem.

The beast continued his growl then barked.

"Easy, Samson," she said.

"Can you control him?" Bryce asked.

*"Warten!"* She commanded Samson to wait.

Sierra had used German words for her commands when she trained Samson because it was easier for Samson to differentiate the commands from her every day communications. The dog did as he was trained to do but he continued to growl.

"I'm going to check it out," Bryce said. "Get behind that nine-passenger van."

*"Hier."* Here, she commanded Samson. The dog whined then moved close to Sierra.

Sierra grabbed Bryce's arm and squeezed, tugging him back. "Bryce, be careful."

Her tone was intense, and something else in her voice told him she did still care deeply about him.

But neither of them would act on that, each having their own reasons.

Gunfire exploded.

The bullet whizzed by his ear even as he shoved Sierra to the ground. She held firm to Samson who wanted to take off. *"Nein!"*

"Sierra, we could use his help here." Bryce edged away from her, preparing to make a run for it and get this guy.

"I won't send him in there to be shot and killed," she said. "I've seen that happen before. I won't do it."

"Then don't. Let's take cover." They were still too exposed.

They crept behind a van they could use for a temporary barrier. Sierra kept her dog close. Bryce could breathe a little easier now that they had some protection—but they weren't out of danger yet. He didn't want to get pinned here. "Contact your sheriff and let him know we have an active shooter."

Sierra nodded and tugged out her cell. She wasn't wearing her radio. She spoke quickly into the cell letting dispatch know about the shooter at the edge of town. Good thing the festivalgoers were mostly at the other end of town near the vendor booths.

Bryce and Sierra had both pulled their weapons out. Another shot rang out and Samson was eager to work. If he weren't well trained, he would already have taken off.

"Cover me." Bryce prepared to dash across the street.

"No, wait!" Sierra whispered. "Don't go out there."

"This is our chance to get him, Sierra."

"You're not law enforcement anymore, Bryce. Remember? You can't arrest that guy even if you catch him. I'm the deputy sheriff. I need to come with you if you go."

Bryce wanted to give her a piece of his mind, but this wasn't the time. They'd have to work together then. As much as he didn't want her in the line of fire, he knew she wasn't going to back down.

Another shot rang out, this time from a different position. Pain stabbed through Bryce.

\* \* \*

"Bryce!" Sierra shouted. Fear coursed through her.

He'd been shot. Bryce stumbled back. Then grabbed his upper arm. He lifted his bloody hand to stare at the wound. "It's just a graze. I'm all right."

"How do you know that? You can't tell by looking at the blood on your hand."

He moved his arm, though with a grimace. "See? It's just a graze." They moved out of harm's way and he peered around the vehicle, his weapon at the ready.

"Well, the sheriff knows where we are, someone should be here soon." Sierra's voice shook.

"Stay here with Samson. You're not going with me. Raul wants you dead, remember? I don't need to worry about you or Samson getting shot."

Oh, that was a low blow. Bryce knew she would want to protect Samson.

"Does he have a command for guarding you?" Bryce asked.

"Of course he does. I'll be fine. I just need *you* to be safe too, Bryce."

Wind whipped around the vehicles and sliced through her like a frozen knife, and of course—the snow had to pick up.

And just like that, Bryce disappeared around the vehicle and ran across the street.

*Grrrrr!*

Sierra got on her cell again for dispatch. "Where's the sheriff? Is he on his way? Or a deputy or something. One of those state officers. Bryce is chasing after the shooter."

"Aren't *you* a deputy?"

"That's beside the point. I don't want to put Samson at more risk from a bullet by chasing after the shooter." She didn't use him as anything but a SAR dog. And sure, if someone broke into her home with intentions to harm her, then Samson was there to guard her, but that didn't mean she'd deliberately put him in harm's way. And yet, it didn't sit right to let Bryce face whoever was out there by himself. Apprehension warred inside—Sierra wasn't sure if she was doing the right thing.

"Sheriff's on his way."

"Okay. Tell him to hurry."

Samson yanked on his leash, pulled her away from the van. He wanted to follow Bryce to track and find the threat per his original K-9 training. That, and Samson was protective like any dog, wanting to neutralize the threat.

*"Sitzen!"* Samson followed her command and sat next to her, his huge form giving her

warmth. *"Zei Brav,"* she said, then again in English: "Good boy."

After a few seconds ticked by, Sierra tightened her hold on Samson's leash. *"Hier.* Come on. I'm taking you home. I need to go after Bryce." Just what Bryce wouldn't want. "From now on, you're wearing your vest when we go out."

Because of his enormous size, Samson had to have a special vest created for him. That had been back in Boulder—over a year earlier. Now that she thought about it, his vest probably wouldn't fit him anymore. They made their way quickly down the street back toward the toy store. Only a few people were out visiting restaurants in this cold. The vendor exhibits still open were at the far end of town.

No one reacted as if they'd heard gunfire.

Samson barked again, letting her know his displeasure. He was well trained. Samson could track the shooter, but she knew what could happen to him as well.

Raul would shoot and kill Samson.

As for Bryce, she couldn't control him. He was a grown man—and he was fully trained in dealing with dangerous criminals. Samson couldn't shoot back or protect himself against a deadly bullet. She pushed through the deepening snow, heading back toward the toy store as fast as she could. And away from Bryce.

*Lord, please, please keep him safe.*

She didn't like that he'd run off from her, and later on she would scold him for it. But only after he was back and safe. She started around to the back, which was the entrance she usually took with Samson, then remembered the woods—the same woods Bryce had probably entered to find the shooter. She'd assured him she wouldn't take that route.

Sierra took Samson through the front of the toy store to the apartment in back and found Dad still watching his program. He glanced up at her. "That was a short walk. Did Bryce go back to his hotel?"

"Dad, didn't you hear those shots fired?"

He turned the television down. "What'd you say?"

Right. "Never mind. I have to go back out. Keep an eye on Samson for me, okay?"

"Always do."

Samson growled then barked at her. He wanted to come along. He nipped at her gloved hands as if he would keep her from going back outside without him. She pressed a kiss on his massive forehead. "You're a good boy. You know what's going on, don't you?"

Her weapon tucked away, she exited through the front, locking all doors behind her. The sheriff met her at the door. Great timing, but she nearly ran into him.

"I got the message about the shots fired. I couldn't find you so hoped you were back here," he said.

"Where's Bryce?" she asked.

"I didn't see him. Tell me what's happened."

"Walk with me while we talk." The snow was growing deep enough to slow them down, filling her with frustration. "Someone took a couple of shots at us while we were out walking the dog. Bryce went after the shooter."

"And you let him go by himself?"

"I tried to stop him. He wanted me to take Samson back home, which I did."

"The dog could find the shooter. Maybe take him down too."

"Yes, and the dog could also get shot and killed. I don't have Samson for these kinds of circumstances, Sheriff." Even though the fear of an attacker was the exact reason she'd wanted a big dog. "Samson is trained for mountain search and rescue."

In response, the sheriff merely offered her a severe frown. Clearly he didn't agree with the way she used her dog. Sierra didn't care what he thought.

Samson wasn't an employee of the sheriff's department. No one other than Sierra had any right to say what he should or shouldn't face.

She tugged her weapon out. She hoped the shooter hadn't taken Bryce out already. Her heart ached at the mere thought of it. And if Bryce got seriously injured out there—how much of the blame lay with her?

"Now are you going to help me then?" she asked. "Because I'm not sitting this one out."

Sheriff Locke readied his own weapon. "That, I am."

# FOUR

Bryce continued following the footsteps through the nearly thigh-deep snow. With the way the snow was falling, soon the tracks left behind would be completely gone.

The snow was to his knees, and hip-deep in some places. He tried to step into the shooter's steps to ease his efforts, but it was still slow going. Without snowshoes, he had no hope of picking up the pace, and this kind of exertion was going to exhaust him too quickly. He wasn't out of shape but navigating the snow-covered rocky terrain took all his effort and focus.

Bryce stopped to catch his breath and take in his surroundings. It was pitch black out here. The only illumination came from the town lights that reflected from the clouds. That reflection helped him to see the way, but it wasn't nearly enough to let him track down the man who had shot him.

What was Bryce doing out here?

This seemed like a suicide mission.

Standing beneath the low-hanging branches of a spruce tree, he considered his options. If he didn't silence his gasps for breath they would give him away—that is, if someone was watching and waiting for the chance to take Bryce out. Except Bryce had no doubt the shooter had come for Sierra specifically and taking Bryce out would simply be a bonus.

Anger coiled in his gut. He couldn't let Raul get to Sierra. His efforts might fall short, but he wouldn't stop trying.

He drew in a sharp, cold breath. Bryce wouldn't give up so easily.

Even though Raul wasn't the typical perp.

Shoving from the spruce tree, Bryce continued following the tracks before it was too late and the shooter was gone for good.

He pushed harder and hiked farther than he thought he could. Finally the snow clouds thinned, allowing the moon to illuminate the forest into an eerie, foreboding scene.

Glancing back, Bryce noticed Crescent Springs was growing smaller. He was putting himself in danger by going deeper into the cold without proper clothing. He wasn't prepared to face off against the elements.

But he'd only been thinking about getting his hands on Raul, ending this once and for all so Sierra could be safe.

He caught a glimpse of the mountains that stood watch over the small tourist town. Bryce flexed his cold fingers in both hands to shake the stiffness away. He wished he'd worn ski bibs instead of jeans layered with thermals. He hadn't thought through what having dinner with Sierra would look like—and he certainly hadn't expected the evening to end this way, with Raul taking a shot at her.

Bryce should have been better prepared.

Regardless, he couldn't stay out here much longer.

The clack of tree trunks rustling with the wind drew his attention to the south. A crunching sound followed. Was Raul pushing on too now that he knew Bryce would follow?

Frustration boiled through him and warmed him—good.

Just a little farther. *God, the tracks are here for me to follow. Help me find this guy before he hurts Sierra!*

He allowed the hot anger to fuel his steps.

A shadow moved in the trees ahead of him. *Yes!*

Bryce was catching up. His weapon ready, he prepared to pull the trigger.

He aimed at the silhouette of a man in the trees. "Stop, police!"

Only he wasn't the police anymore. Old habits die hard.

His prey fled deeper into the woods. He was so close! Bryce would get his hands on Raul. Adrenaline pushed him farther and deeper.

A force slammed into his body. The breath whooshed from him. He crashed face-first into the biting snow that rushed into his mouth and nose.

Bryce fought for purchase, grappling with the snow. Reaching for something, anything, to push the weight from him. He twisted around to face the barrel of a weapon.

Reflex kicked in.

Bryce rolled as gunfire blasted into the space where he'd been mere seconds before. Using his training, he knocked the weapon from the man's hand. Kicked his attacker to the ground as he twisted away and scrambled to his feet, despite the snow impeding his efforts. Bryce searched, digging through the snow and found his weapon. Gasping for breath, he shoved the fear down.

Aiming his weapon, he turned in a circle looking for Raul.

*No.*

*No, no, no.*

Bryce had lost him. He'd fled into the night again. Bryce could follow the tracks farther, but the cold was making him numb and slowing both his moving and thinking. Grousing that he'd let the man get the best of him and get away on top of it, he decided to follow the footprints left behind. The cold seeped through his inadequate clothes all the way to his bones. From now on, he'd dress for unexpected treks through snow on cold winter nights. Maybe even drag snowshoes around with him so he'd be prepared.

He took one more step.

A crack resounded directly under his feet—a familiar and terrifying sound.

He stilled and listened. Gurgling water. A river? A stream? Whatever it was, he'd just stepped on the thin layer of ice covering moving water—thin and dangerous.

Another crack and then his foot plunged into the icy water.

Sierra heard the snap and the plunge into water that came after.

*Oh, no!*

"Bryce!" she shouted.

Gasping for breath, she pushed forward through the snow, following his tracks. She'd seen a man standing there not fifteen yards away through the trees. She had just decided it was Bryce at the moment he'd stepped on the ice.

Now she couldn't see him at all. "We have to hurry!" she shouted to the sheriff who trailed her.

"Bryce, I'm coming." She pushed faster, breathing cold hair into her lungs.

"We're on our way!" Sheriff Locke shouted. "Hold on!"

Holding on when you fell into a frozen river wasn't always an option. *Oh, Lord, please let us reach him in time!*

She hiked as fast as she could, wishing she could push faster. "Answer me, Bryce!"

Another splash of water resounded.

"No!" Sierra cried out.

Then she was at the river that weaved through these woods. It was wide and deep enough to be lethal.

Bryce was clinging to a frozen branch as more ice gave away again beneath him. He held tight…for now. She knew that he would soon succumb to hypothermia and would no longer be able to hold himself up on that branch.

"Stay back." His voice was commanding,

but she heard the hint of fear. The shivering in his words.

That sound shook her to the core.

"No." She crawled along the thick snow-covered branch and scooted along until she reached him. The sheriff found a boulder nearby so he wouldn't risk stepping through the ice. Together they hefted Bryce up and out of the river.

They dragged him away from the riverbank. "Are you okay?" she asked. "Scratch that. It's a stupid question. Let's get you back."

He wasn't out of danger yet.

Shivering, he gasped for breath. "Thank you. But you shouldn't—"

"Let's get you back." Sheriff Locke's voice was authoritative. No nonsense.

As was Sierra. "Of course we should have. Now, let's go and get you warm."

"But he's still out there. Raul is still out there." Bryce teeth chattered. "I can't let him get to you."

What was it about Bryce that made him feel personally responsible for protecting her from Raul? It confounded her and warmed her heart at the same time. But she needed to stick to the no-nonsense attitude. Experience had taught her it was the best way to push past his stubbornness.

"I'll get more deputies," the sheriff offered. "We'll follow the tracks until we find him, Bryce. In the meantime, you're going to freeze to death if you don't get out of those clothes."

"Sheriff Locke," she said. "It's too treacherous to go after Raul at night. You see what happened to Bryce. He almost got swept away in the river. You can't send deputies out there after him."

The sheriff growled. "I'll let the state boys know and we'll see if they want to join in the search tonight. He's too close to let get away. We all know the risks. Leaving him out there is also a risk."

"I agree. That's a big risk to Sierra." Bryce forced the words out through his shivers.

Sierra didn't want to argue with the two of them. They had a point, but the danger was real to anyone who was going to search for him in this terrain on a cold snowy night.

She kept her mouth shut as they hiked the rest of the way back to town, Bryce between them. His legs weren't moving too well—numb and cold—and he was unstable on his feet.

What if they hadn't followed him? What then? Bryce would have died out there tonight.

"Are you sure it was Novack?" Sheriff Locke finally asked.

"I fought with him. But I didn't get a look at his face. It was too dark and happened too fast. But it must have been the same man who attacked Sierra today in town. Who else could it have been tonight?" Bryce's words slurred as his body grew colder. "I shouldn't have let him get the best of me."

"Need I remind you that you're not law enforcement? You should have waited on me and my men or the state officers in town."

"Do we have to talk about this now?" Sierra asked. She wanted to get Bryce somewhere warm before it was too late and frostbite took his legs or worse. The sheriff could wait until later to dress him down. But he seemed to disagree as he continued his scolding.

"You can't go chasing people through the woods and think you're going to detain them."

"I might not have the power of the law behind a badge," Bryce said again through chattering teeth. "But you can bet I'll detain them."

Sheriff Locke finally chuckled. "At least you're single-minded. I wouldn't stand in your way, honestly. Just doing my duty to remind you to keep it legal. I can't really say I object to you trying to keep our town safe. My department is spread thin with this ice festival.

And we certainly don't need a shooter scaring off tourists from our one claim to fame."

Sierra thought they would never make it to the toy store. The cold had seeped into her bones so much her hands shook as she fumbled to unlock the door.

"I think we should get him to the clinic," Sheriff Locke suggested.

"They're not open this late."

"They are with the festival. Let Doc make sure he's okay."

"I'm fine, I'm fine. I just need to get warm." He started to cross the street.

"Where do you think you're going?" she asked.

"To my hotel room."

She grabbed him and swung him back around. "Oh, no, you don't. Not until I've made sure you're going to be okay."

The sheriff took this opening to back away. "Call me if you need anything, Sierra. I'm going to let the other agencies know about what happened tonight. We might start combing the woods soon. But you stay here. I don't want you out there. Understand?" He gave her a pointed look.

"Sure." She focused back on Bryce as the sheriff left them.

"I'm soaked through," he said. "I need new clothes and those are in my room at the hotel."

Despite his protests, he let her lead him through the store and into the back apartment.

She ushered him next to the fireplace. "Dad has a pair of pants you can borrow while we dry those," she said. "And I'm going to take a look at your arm. If it's more than a graze, then you are going to the clinic after all. Do you hear me?"

Bryce said nothing. Concern crawled over her. She should force him to go see a doctor anyway.

Dad rose from the recliner. Samson sniffed Bryce and released a low groan.

"What happened?" Dad asked. "Don't tell me you—"

"He took a tumble, that's all," she said and gave Dad a warning look.

"You don't need to sugarcoat it," Bryce said. "I fell through the ice."

Dad's eyes widened. "You—"

"Dad. Will you please get Bryce some clothes?"

Dad nodded. "All right. Can you follow me?"

"Sure," Bryce said through gritted teeth.

Was he trying to hide the chattering?

Dad led him upstairs to his bedroom. Now that both men were out of sight, Sierra collapsed into a chair, pressed her face into her arms on the table.

"Oh, Lord," she whispered. Raul was in town and closing in. He was after her.

Samson nudged her and whined. She weaved her fingers through his fur and held on tight. Held on for dear life. Would this ever end?

If and when it did, would she survive? Would the people around her get hurt—or even killed? Bryce shouldn't be here putting himself in harm's way for her. Somehow she needed to find the strength to push him away for his safety, and that of her heart.

# FIVE

Sierra's dad had laid out a few pairs of jeans and shirts on the bed for Bryce to try. Bryce held the clothes up and looked at them. They would do. His limbs, hands and feet were finally starting to feel normal again, though he still shivered. He wished he could take a hot shower first. That's why he'd wanted to go back to his own room.

Woulda. Coulda. Shoulda.

But he took Sierra's urging him along with her into her own home as a sign that she didn't want him to leave her. He shared the sentiment. Raul was still out there. He'd come close again tonight. More worrisome was that Raul had made two attempts on her life in one day.

That would be enough to set anyone on edge.

Sierra wanted protection though she wouldn't admit it. And it certainly seemed like they were safer when they were together.

She'd saved him—pulled him from the icy river. She and Sheriff Locke—for which Bryce was grateful.

It was like before. Bryce and Sierra had saved each other.

He shook off the ruminations, the reassurances that he was doing the right thing by staying, and focused on getting ready and back out there to protect Sierra.

In the bathroom in John's room, Bryce washed up the bullet graze and found bandages in the cabinet. A couple of millimeters in the wrong direction and he would have needed a medical professional's attention. He could only be grateful it hadn't come to that—that he hadn't been left with an injury that would take a long while to treat or heal, something for which he had no time. He couldn't get distracted.

His coat had been ripped so he'd need to patch it or replace it soon.

Finished dressing, a look in the mirror told him what he already knew—his lips were a little blue, and he was still much too cold.

A knock came at the door. "How you doing in there?" John asked.

"I'm almost done. Coming out."

He opened the door.

Crossing his arms, John eyed him. "Sierra

made some hot chocolate. Go sit by the fire. She said you're not going anywhere tonight. I don't know if that's because she wants to make sure you're not going to die from hypothermia, or if it has to do with the gunshots she mentioned earlier. Sooner or later, one of you is going to tell me what's going on. I try not to interfere because she's a deputy here and was law enforcement back in Boulder. My girl can take care of herself, but there's something more going on this time. Sooner rather than later, I'll need some answers."

"That's a deal." Bryce followed him downstairs where he took a seat next to the fireplace and let the warmth wash over him. Finally. Comfort.

Exhaustion warred with his need to remain on high alert. He spotted the English mastiff sitting like a sentinel near the back door that opened up to those woods. Anger burrowed deeper at the thought of Raul, still out there—getting the upper hand and getting away. Bryce wanted to go back out and track through those woods again until he hauled Raul in, but Bryce knew his limits. He was in no condition to do anything else for now. The sheriff made mention of others looking for Raul tonight. He hoped they brought their own tracking dogs and made short work of it, considering that Sierra wouldn't put Samson out there for the task.

As for Samson sitting next to the door as if guarding it, Bryce understood how the dog felt. He wanted to do the same. Right now, the hotel room across the street felt entirely too far from Sierra so he was glad she'd wanted him to stay.

She approached and offered him a mug. He took it and felt the warmth, letting it seep into his palms. Sierra eased into the comfy seat across from him.

Neither of them spoke for a few moments. He must have freezer brain because he couldn't formulate any words. He fought the need to drift off to sleep. He was here with Sierra. He would stay awake for this moment with her.

She peered closely at him. "You're looking better. Your color has improved. I wish you would have let me take you to the clinic."

"You're right. I'm better." Being here with her was all he needed.

"What about the gunshot wound? Was it a graze like you said?"

"Yep. I bandaged it up. I promise, if I need a doctor or the hospital, you'll be the first to know."

Her smile told him she liked what he'd said.

She turned her attention to the fire for a few moments, then looked back at him.

"Go ahead and sleep," she said softly. "Samson's here. He'll warn us if anyone gets close. Besides, I don't think Raul is going to try anything tonight."

"Why not?"

"He's only human, Bryce. He was running from you. He has to be numb with cold too. He needs time to recover. I wonder where he went? Does he have some hideout? Some cabin out there? Maybe he got on a snowmobile and took off and is miles away by now. Who knows. But while you were upstairs, I talked to Sheriff Locke. He said the state will be bringing in dogs again tomorrow. It takes time to get fresh and rested dogs here—unfortunately, this terrain wears them down quickly. But until they arrive, law agencies are all on high alert. So for tonight, Bryce, I think we're as safe as we're going to be."

He wished he could fully trust in that. Then again, this might be the last decent rest he got for a good long while, and he needed to make the most of it so he could be at his best. "I should go back to—"

"No. You can sleep on the sofa right there. For tonight. You and Samson. I know you won't sleep if you're not here."

"You know me that well, do you?"

Her eyes shimmered in the firelight and an emotion he couldn't quite pin down surfaced in her gaze. His heart melted a little.

"I do, actually." She kept her voice low. "I know you have a protective nature."

Sierra held his gaze for a few heartbeats, then she suddenly stood and broke the moment. "I'll bring down some bedding. Sheets, a pillow and comforter. Samson will stand guard."

Funny that she'd let Samson do that now when she sure hadn't wanted him tracking a shooter. But Bryce understood that. It was the whole reason she'd broken things off with Bryce to begin with.

She didn't want anyone else she loved getting killed.

After getting ready for bed, Sierra fluffed her pillows so she could sit up and read her Bible, hoping the comfort of the words would wipe out the events of the day. Her Bible fell open to Second Samuel and she started reading the prophet, her gaze holding at chapter twenty-two, verse three. "The God of my rock; in Him will I trust: He is my shield, and the horn of my salvation, my high tower, and my refuge, my savior. Thou savest me from violence."

The words were just what she needed to read, what her heart needed to hear. She closed her eyes and meditated on the scripture.

*You've saved me from violence before, God. Please save me from Raul.*

She hated that the man's proximity could set her on edge and fill her with fear.

Sierra wanted to trust God to save her, but images of Raul wouldn't leave her mind. She set her Bible down and turned off the bedside lamp, then she crept to the window to peer out at the street below. Her second-floor room was right above the toy store so she looked out onto Main Street. At this hour a few street lamps stood lonely in the night illuminating snow piled high in the street and on the sidewalk. Early in the morning a snowplow would wake her up, creating berms along the sidewalk. She would need to get out there and shovel it away so potential customers could get to the store.

Dad had pulled her aside after she'd left Bryce downstairs with Samson. Her father had wanted full disclosure about what was going on, and she'd shared what she could without including the sordid details. Just that someone she'd put away was trying to get to her.

Seeing the pain on his face had nearly done her in. On the other hand, she needed to tell him so he could be on alert. It was one thing to be attacked in Boulder. Quite another to have the Novack brothers come here to her home. What if Damien had survived and both brothers had come after her and caught her off guard? Dad could have gotten hurt too. Anyone close to her.

A chill crept over her and she rubbed her arms.

Sierra climbed back in bed and thought back to Bryce's face tonight as he sat by the fire. She'd always found him attractive and so caring. He'd come here for her.

*For me...*

Why did he still have to care?

She didn't want him to be caught in the crossfire of Raul's attempt to get at her. Sierra was scared for Bryce. As scared for him as she was herself, Dad and anyone else close to her.

She knew how to stay safe and now she had a guard dog that weighed more than the average man. But Sierra didn't want Samson hurt either.

*God, what do I do?*

She wasn't only confused about the dangerous situation. Bryce walking back in her life stirred all sorts of long-buried feelings in her heart. She wanted him here, and yet she wished he hadn't shown up.

She'd gone to a lot of trouble to put both time and distance between them.

Her reasons for coming back home and leaving Boulder behind were many. Dousing the remnants of feelings for Bryce was among those reasons. Did he know that?

An image of an exhausted Bryce relaxing in the chair by her fire stayed with her much too long, until finally she felt herself dozing and she allowed sleep to take her.

*There was a noise. A subtle nuance, or a feeling, she wasn't sure, but something stirred her from a deep sleep. She blinked her eyes open. Turned her head to the right. The clock on the table read 2:30 a.m. She slowly reached toward the drawer in the bedside table where she kept her Boulder PD–issued weapon—a Glock 22. She slowly and quietly slid the drawer open and reached in. She felt no cold plastic against her fingers. She felt around the drawer. Her pulse jumped.*

*Her gun was gone.*

*Heart pounding, she pushed up from the bed. She always put the gun right there in the side table and now it was missing. What was going on? In her mind she retraced her steps last night. Exhausted, she'd dragged herself to bed much too late and after a little while of tossing and turning, she'd taken something to help her fall asleep. And yes...she'd put her Glock in the drawer like always.*

*Alarms resounded in her head. Realization dawned as fear corded her neck and tightened, choking her.*

*She had to breathe. Had to get air.*

*Someone was in her apartment.*

*Had that someone taken her weapon?*

*She grabbed her cell to call 911 and slipped over to the corner to get the baseball bat she kept there. It was her dad's weapon of choice and had been her protection for many years. That training had never left her. She reached for the bat to slip her fingers around the slender neck.*

*Arms grabbed her from behind and squeezed hard.*

*A raspy voice whispered in her ear. "You put my brother away and now you're going to pay."*

What to do. What to do. Push away the panic. Stay calm. *"I don't know what you're talking about."*

*"Damien Novack is my brother. He asked me to take care of you."*

*Sierra twisted out of his grip only to look down the muzzle of a gun.* Her *gun. It was loaded, too—she knew because she kept it loaded. The gun was of no use without bullets. And it was of no use to her in someone else's hands. She could think about her failures later. Right now, she had to survive.*

*"What... What do you want?" A stupid question to extend her life only a few moments more. She knew what he'd come for.*

*Raul punched her in the face. Dazed, she couldn't respond as he threw her onto the bed. He aimed her own weapon at her. She rolled as he pulled the trigger, the sound firing off in her ears, hammering forever in her head.*

Sierra shot up in bed, a noise startling her awake. Gasping for breath she saw the lamp on the floor. Had she knocked it off? Was that the noise she'd heard? She couldn't be sure. She reached for her weapon.

Her door burst open and she screamed. Bryce and her father rushed in, both of them wielding weapons. Air whooshed from her. Samson rushed into the room, a vicious warning bark escaping his maw. She reached for him and his wet tongue licked her face. "Shh. It's okay."

"Are you all right?" Bryce lowered his weapon.

"Yes. It was just… It was just a nightmare."

A vivid memory from that night. She'd never been the same.

"All right. Somebody want to tell me what's going on? And I mean the whole truth this time."

*Oh, Dad…*

# SIX

Bryce put his weapon away and exhaled. He scraped his hand over his eyes. He wanted to rush to Sierra and hold her, but he held back. Instead he locked gazes with her.

Understanding passed between them and he read it clearly in her eyes—she'd had a nightmare about Raul and what had happened the night that he had broken into her home and accosted her. Raul had targeted her because she'd been instrumental in securing Damien's incarceration, with a life sentence.

What Bryce couldn't know was if she'd been having this same nightmare all along since that night years ago. Or had recent events triggered the nightmare tonight?

He could understand if they had.

But hearing her scream when he'd finally nodded off had been like a stab to his heart. He could have died from a heart attack at the panic he'd felt before he'd gotten upstairs to her room. It didn't help that he'd been in the middle of his own dream. He couldn't recall the details only that it had left him disturbed.

John stared at them both now, waiting for an explanation. Bryce wasn't at liberty to share more than Sierra wanted her father to know.

"I'll leave you two alone," he said. "Come on, Samson."

Samson understood Bryce's command, but he didn't seem happy about it. The dog whined and refused to budge. He was loyal to Sierra not Bryce.

Bryce looked at Sierra. "You want him to stay? You might feel safer with him in the room with you."

"I'd feel safer if Samson was guarding the entryways." Sierra sighed and urged Samson to leave with Bryce. "*Aus…* Out, Samson." She stood and urged Samson out the door with Bryce, leaning out the door to whisper, "I guess I'll have that talk with Dad now."

Bryce nodded. "I can stay if you like."

"It's okay." Grief filled her eyes, concern for her father's reaction obviously overshadowing any remnants of the terror her nightmare had ushered in.

The bedroom door shut. Bryce stared down at Samson. The dog's massive forehead was wrinkled as if he was worried about John's reaction too. Bryce rubbed the dog behind the ears. "I know, boy, I know. Let's go downstairs to make sure the bogeyman doesn't get in."

He followed Samson as the big dog plodded down the steps. On the first floor, Bryce checked the windows and the doors to make sure all remained locked, then poured himself a glass of milk. Samson's water bowl was filled with water, so Bryce poured milk in a separate small bowl for Samson too.

While he finished off the milk and Samson lapped his up, Bryce thought back to the years Sierra spent raising and training Samson for work as a K-9. Strange how things had unfolded—that despite all of Samson's training, she was afraid to put him in harm's way.

The milk finished, Bryce washed up the glass and bowl, and then he sat back on the sofa and gave Samson some more petting and attention. At the same time, he thought about the conversation Sierra was having with her father, and prayed for that discussion to go well. Her father had to realize as a police officer and then a detective, Sierra had faced some life-threatening situations. But how would he react to the severity of the danger facing her now?

The big dog tried to sneak up onto the sofa

with Bryce. His size wouldn't allow for that. From the guilty look on the animal's face, Bryce was sure that Sierra had trained him to stay off the furniture.

"You think you can get away with it because I'm a softy?" Bryce rubbed Samson's ears and prevented his slow climb onto the couch. Samson finally settled on the floor at Bryce's feet.

Bryce had almost nodded off when Sierra appeared at the bottom of the stairs and drew his attention.

"You're still up." She came all the way into the small space. "The fire is almost out."

She bent to grab more logs.

"Leave it. It's fine. Tell me. How did it go?" He ran his hand through his hair.

Samson was spread out on the floor now and sighed.

She crossed her arms. Instead of moving closer or sitting on the sofa next to him or the chair, she kept her distance. "As you would expect. He was angry and hurt about the whole thing."

She swiped at her cheeks. "I'd wanted to protect him from all that. I'd wanted to escape to a more peaceful way of life and now Raul has brought the fear and chaos here to Crescent Springs." Anger edged her tone.

Bryce understood just how she felt. He hated that this had happened. It was why he'd wanted to catch up to Raul tonight. If he had, maybe this would all be over, and Sierra and John could get back to their lives. "Sierra, I need to talk to you about something. I don't want to keep you up too late, but now seems like the right time."

"I don't think I'm going to go to sleep anytime soon anyway." She finally eased into the chair across from the sofa. "What's wrong?"

"It's not so much that anything's wrong, but tonight, when someone was shooting at us, you wanted to protect Samson. I understand that. But he's a big dog. He's trained to do many things—including protect. Remember you trained him to become part of the new BPD's K-9 unit. Tonight you were afraid to let him protect you or to let him go after Raul." He wasn't telling her anything she didn't already know.

He wanted to better understand her reasons.

Sierra stared into the dying embers as though gathering her thoughts, or softening angry words she might have said. "I just couldn't put him in danger, Bryce. I know it sounds ludicrous. Maybe I should have let him go. I'm sorry. I put you in greater danger instead."

"It's all right. That's not why I'm bringing it up. I'd just like to understand."

"Samson and I trained with another dog—a German shepherd named Jackson—and his handler, Officer Kimmie Tombs. We worked hard with them and learned so much." Then the tears came and she once again swiped at her face. "Jackson become a K-9. He and Kimmie were called upon that very first week that he was official. He… Jackson was shot and killed."

Sierra looked at him then.

Bryce understood better now. He'd known about this, of course, but not how much it affected her. "It was that next week you resigned."

"And moved to Crescent Springs."

Samson stirred and sat up, then shifted his big head over to Sierra. She grabbed him around his neck to hug him. "Here he works as a SAR dog only and we train every day. Twice a month we get with other handlers and their mountain rescue dogs for training. It's been good for both of us. He's still useful, still helping people—just not in the way we thought he would back then."

She pulled Samson's face up to look at her. His big tongue lolled as drool spilled out both sides of his mouth. Sierra wiped it away with one of the drool towels she kept on the side table. "He loves it here. You love it here, don't you, boy?"

He barked.

Sierra chuckled. "Shh. Don't wake Dad. I hope he could even fall asleep after what I told him. But now he'll appreciate Samson that much more."

Not if Sierra didn't allow the dog to protect her.

Her gaze slid to Bryce. "We won't let Raul come after us or cause us to live in fear, Bryce. We're going to find him and bring him in."

"We are?"

"Yes. You, me—and yes, Samson. We'll go out and search for him. We know these mountains pretty well, don't we, Samson?"

"That could be dangerous, Sierra. Raul is after you. That might be just what he wants—for you to come out after him."

"Better than letting him come here and get me. We'll have the element of surprise as our advantage."

While he liked the way she thought, it didn't make his self-appointed task of protecting her easier.

The next morning Sierra struggled to stay alert as she helped her father get ready to open up the store. She set up the cash drawer in the register while he arranged building block sets from a shipment they'd received last week. They were so behind!

She yawned and rubbed her eyes, unsure if they would ever catch up. But she could do only so much. What would have happened to the store if she hadn't come to help Dad last year? He was too stubborn to hire more help than Jane, thinking he could do it all himself. When Sierra had come home for a week to visit him after the K-9 dog Jackson had been killed, she'd been devastated and brought Samson to Crescent Springs. When she got there, boxes of toys were actually in the aisles, left there to be dealt with who knew when. Add to that, Dad couldn't seem to balance the drawer at the end of the day. He wasn't worried about it, but Sierra had been. That week-long visit had been the nudging she'd needed to leave Boulder. Leave it all behind. That's when she'd decided to stay.

Save Samson from a similar fate to Jackson.

Help Dad with the store.

Dad needed help and Sierra had needed a big change.

A grunt from the aisle brought her attention back to the present. She should finish up the drawer and help Dad with those boxes.

This afternoon she was on deputy duty. What task would the sheriff assign her given the ongoing ice festival? She'd been here in Crescent Springs as a deputy during the last festival. A couple of guys had gotten rowdy after too much to drink—spectators rather than participants—but other than that one incident, things had gone smoothly.

Sierra sighed and shoved the cash register closed. Her hands trembled. She stared at them. Squeezed them closed. Opened them. Squeezed. Opened.

Still shaking.

The nightmare last night had prevented much-needed sleep and set her on edge when she needed to stay sharp until Raul was behind bars once again. Instead, she was irritable and cranky. And Dad had hardly spoken to her this morning.

After all, she'd told him the whole story last night.

She wasn't sure if he was upset with her or just needed time to process what had happened in his own way. As for Bryce, he'd insisted on taking Samson for his morning walk, and had returned the dog already, before leaving her at the store with her father so he could head across the street to his hotel room to shower and dress.

All of this before the store opened. Jane should be here at any moment to help.

Sierra moved to the storage room to bring a few more boxes of toys out. She hefted a box and tried to maneuver through the door but failed and the box toppled, spilling fidget toys everywhere. Sierra pressed her forehead against the wall and groaned.

The Novack brothers' escape and plane crash had certainly turned her world upside down, and now she wasn't sure which end was up.

She knelt and reloaded the toys in the box as she thought about Bryce. She'd been stunned to see him in the store yesterday. His sudden reappearance in her life left her confused. After all, she'd put enough time and distance between them with her move from Boulder to Crescent Springs, she should have doused any remnants of feelings she had for him.

Maybe if he'd stayed away, those feelings could have lain buried forever, but it was as though they had simply been dormant and all it had taken was his presence for them to stir back to life.

For a few moments last night she'd watched him sitting on the sofa dozing, Samson at his feet, as the fire died. Warm sensations and longing had flooded her. She would be the first one to admit that she was definitely missing that kind of warmth in her everyday life, but she'd denied herself that relationship with him because of the danger. She wouldn't love a cop or anyone in a dangerous line of work again.

Sierra hefted the refilled box of fidget toys on her hip and lugged the merchandise through the store in search of Dad.

The sound of boxes toppling caught her attention. "Dad?" she moved to the left of the store. Boxes had spilled into the main aisle. "Dad. You okay?"

"Yep," he grumbled from behind a display. "Sorry."

"No reason to be sorry. I dropped this box all over the floor just a minute ago. Looks like we're both having the same kind of morning." She set her box down and blew out a breath. "We could wait until Jane gets here. She can arrange the toys and stock the shelves."

"I can do it." He didn't even look at her. Just started picking up the toys. So he was upset with her after all.

Sierra couldn't take it. "Dad, I'm sorry, okay? I'm sorry I didn't tell you. I just wanted to spare you. Please don't be mad at me. It just makes everything that much worse."

She helped him gather all the toys and stack the boxes in silence. Then Dad straightened to his full height, finally looking her in the eyes. "I'm not mad at you. Not anymore. I just wish I could help protect you. I feel... helpless."

Sierra started to reach for him, grab him up in a hug. She needed to know things were okay between them, but the door jingled, startling them both. Hadn't he locked the door after Bryce left for his hotel earlier?

*Oh, Dad...* She wanted to comfort him. "We'll talk more about this later," she whispered.

She started to move, but he grabbed her arm. "Let me see who it is first."

Sierra frowned and shook her head. "You—" Then she caught herself. If this was what he needed to feel like he was protecting her, then she wouldn't deny him.

Dad stepped from the aisle as if he would defend her from an attacker. She told herself that there wasn't really anything to worry about. Raul wouldn't actually walk through the front door of a toy store to come for her... Would he?

A chill ran over her. She heard the footfalls but could see Dad's shoulders relax.

"Who is it, Dad?" She hoped it wasn't a

customer. The store wasn't due to open for another half an hour and she sure needed that to compose herself.

"Morning, Sheriff." Dad left her standing in the aisle while he stepped forward to greet her boss.

"Morning. I need to see Sierra."

Dad turned to stare at her where she'd remained in the aisle. "Any news on that escaped convict?"

"That's what I came to talk about."

She spotted a fidget toy they'd missed, and grabbed it and held on to it. Maybe she could use it to keep herself awake, despite the fatigue digging deeper into her bones. Sierra moved to the counter. Sheriff Locke was making his way toward her.

His gaze landed on her.

He looked her up and down, taking her in, and she didn't think he'd missed the look of a woman who hadn't slept much. The sheriff frowned. "Where's your bodyguard?"

"Samson's barking in the back, don't you hear him?"

"Samson should be up here with you. Wherever you are, keep the dog with you. But I wasn't referring to Samson."

"Oh, you mean Bryce." Had the sheriff figured she knew whom he'd meant to begin with?

"Sheriff, I don't need a bodyguard. I'm trained law enforcement, which you already know."

"Even a trained law enforcement officer is vulnerable with a target on her back. I don't want to feel like I neglected one of my deputies, but you know the ice festival is our busy time so between you and me, I'm glad he's here for you. Take advantage of that."

She sighed. "With law enforcement coming down around these mountains to look for Raul, surely he'll be caught soon."

"For all our sakes I hope you're right."

"Where could he possibly hide?" The question sounded ridiculous. She risked a look at the sheriff.

He'd arched a brow and she sent him a wry grin. The San Juan Mountains region was filled with millions of acres of forest, old mining camps and probably a few deserted cabins. No one knew that better than her and Samson. But Raul didn't know this area. Could he find his way around that and hide well? She doubted it.

"You said you'd come by to talk about Raul. Do you have any news?"

"Only that the dogs are here." He frowned and scraped his hand over his mouth. "That is, dogs to track the fugitive. In the meantime, I had hoped I could convince you to take some time off. Go on vacation. Leave Crescent Springs."

Sierra couldn't withhold her stunned look.

"At least until this is over, of course."

"You can't be serious." Samson nearly knocked her over as the dog rushed from their private apartment in back. Dad closed the door and gave the sheriff a smile and a nod. He'd let the dog up into the store. Sierra groaned. Samson was massive and the shelves were heavily stocked. Just one walk down the aisle could end in disaster.

Giving herself a reprieve from the two sets of human eyes pinned on her, she squatted to rub Samson's head and behind his soft floppy ears, focusing her attention on him. Was the sheriff right? Should she leave town? She didn't want to bring danger here to Crescent Springs.

Frustration boiled to the surface, but before hot tears could spill out Samson licked her. She wiped her face with her sleeve. Then finally she stood to face the two men who seemed to be staring her down.

"Look. Maybe I ran from Boulder." Sure she'd used the store and her father's need of help as her excuse, but she knew the real reason. "I'm here now. And I'm not running again. Staying here is the right thing to do. I can't let Raul think he has me running scared." She hoped the men understood. "I won't let what happened in Boulder force me from Crescent Springs as well. You've got my back, Sheriff."

"And the people of this town have got your back too," Dad said. She appreciated his support. At the very least, *he* understood.

Concern for the tourist population that came for the snow sports and ice climbing competition skittered through her, but Raul was here for *her*. Not them.

"Good. That settles it then. I'm staying here in Crescent Springs. For the short-term and the long haul."

"Fine, but you're off duty until this is over and Raul is caught. I don't want you facing off with him under any circumstance if that can be avoided."

Her jaw dropped. A few breaths passed before she composed herself. "Why, Sheriff? You said yourself that we're stretched thin with the festival. You need me to help you. You need me."

"I need you to be safe. This is *me*, protecting you. Since you won't take a few days away from here, I'll do my best to help in other ways and maybe even find this jerk too." He stared at her. "Don't look so surprised, or so grim. It isn't the end of the world, Sierra. Stay safe. Let Bryce help protect you, along with your father, and maybe you'll even consider letting your K-9–trained dog protect you."

"What about… What about SAR? If someone needs—"

"That's different. If someone needs to be found, you and Samson are close. But deputy duties are on hold for now."

Sierra wanted to protest, but she recognized the hard set of Sheriff Locke's jaw and knew he'd made up his mind. She almost wished she was still in Boulder because maybe there, she would be allowed to keep working.

Still, coming back here had been the best decision. The only thing she'd missed about Boulder was Bryce.

She hadn't realized how much until he'd walked back into her life yesterday.

And that kind of thinking would lead nowhere.

The door jingled, startling all three of them—the store wasn't open yet. She or Dad should have locked the front door after the sheriff came in. But they were both much too distracted.

Bryce stood at the entrance for a moment as if to let his vision adjust, then his gaze found hers and seemed to drill through her.

With a somber expression he made his way toward her.

Her heart pounded. Why did she react this way the moment he walked into the room?

# SEVEN

Bryce got the impression he'd interrupted a private conversation between Sierra, her father and Sheriff Locke. But he trudged forward anyway with every intention of inserting himself into the thick of things.

He wouldn't be left out. Not as this juncture.

As he approached the counter, he forced a grin. "You guys are getting started without me?"

Frowning, she shook her head and straightened the pens and cards on the counter. She didn't seem happy with whatever had been discussed. He didn't wait for an explanation and instead gave Samson the attention the dog required. Or rather, demanded. Bryce thought Samson's eyes were scolding him for not staying here this morning after Bryce had taken him for a walk. Like the dog wanted Bryce to stay and help him protect Sierra. "I know, boy, I know."

When he stood, John had moved over near the door, preparing to open it for customers. Someone had already shoveled the sidewalk in front of the stores, and would need to keep at it all day long.

"What did Samson say to you?" Sierra teased.

"He implied with his eyes that he didn't like that I had left him and John here to protect you alone. So he was scolding me. I was just telling him I understand that you need to be watched and protected from Raul." Sierra's eyes had narrowed as he spoke. He lifted his palms in surrender. "I'm just telling you what he said."

Sheriff chuckled. "You two are ridiculous."

"Maybe it's you who needs protecting, Bryce," she said.

"Yeah, from you. I see that look in your eyes," he said. "You want to kick me to the curb right now. But even if you do, I'll stand out there in the cold." He wouldn't let Raul get another chance at her like he had before in Boulder, and then twice already here in Crescent Springs.

Sheriff Locke actually rolled his eyes. "Well that's my cue to leave you two to protect each other, but please remember—I want to know if something suspicious happens. Anything odd or strange or out of the ordinary. Don't take any risks. Let's keep in close contact."

Hmm. That was an interesting way to put it. She was a deputy. Why wouldn't she be in close contact? Bryce didn't miss Sierra stiffening at the sheriff's words.

"Thanks, Sheriff," she said. She didn't exactly seem pleased to see her boss in the store this morning.

Bryce would wait until the sheriff exited before he spoke. Sierra held her silence as well. He hoped she would tell him what was going on. Before she got the chance the front door signaled the sheriff's exit and that someone had entered. Jane came through bringing snow with her on her coat and boots. She coughed then spotted Sierra at the back and gave a sheepish grin. "Sorry I'm late."

"No worries," Sierra said. "It's hectic out there."

Sierra turned to him with a forced smile.

"What was that all about?" he asked.

"That depends on what you're referring to specifically."

After shrugging out of her coat, Jane hung it on a rack at the back wall. She rushed behind the counter and stuffed her bag onto an already overflowing shelf. Tugging off her knit cap, she turned and smiled at them while she finger combed her long black hair and put it up in a hair clip. She released a hefty breath. "There. Do I look like I'm together?"

"As always." Sierra's smile was warm and her gaze held respect for her employee.

Then Sierra turned her attention back to Bryce and grabbed his arm. "Jane if you don't mind working up front and—" she leaned in to whisper "—keeping an eye on Dad, I have a few things to do."

Jane scrunched her face and waved her hand. "Pfft. Go ahead. Please. You're the boss. I got this."

Sierra promptly ushered Bryce and Samson to the apartment. Bryce let her grip on his arm remain as she urged him back like he was a child. At the door to the apartment she seemed to realize she still held on to him and released him.

She opened the door for him. "Gentlemen first."

He tried to hide his smile as he entered her home. This was serious business and he needed to remember that.

Someone was out to kill Sierra.

Once inside, Samson rushed to his water bowl and Bryce stuffed his hands in his pockets. "What's going on? What did I miss?"

She paced frantically and shoved her hands

through her hair. "The sheriff first asked me to leave town for a few days. Then when I refused he said I'm off duty until further notice. What does that even mean?"

*Good for the sheriff.* Bryce approached and blocked her from pacing. He gently grabbed her arms. "Sierra, calm down. It means that he cares about you, and I for one am glad for that since I feel the same way. I came to Crescent Springs to be here for you. Protect you. Investigate. Everything that's needed to make sure you're safe." Oops. He'd said the wrong thing.

"You think this is about you? Me not working as a deputy makes it easier for you to watch out for me?" She shrugged free of his grip, a deep frown brimming with annoyance carved into her forehead.

He dropped his hands. "You're right. I'm sorry that I was selfish enough to think of it that way."

She covered her face with her palms. He couldn't be sure—was she crying? He didn't know what to say to appease her. Maybe he would just go stand outside the door and watch over her from a distance. Maybe that would be better for them both.

She dropped her hands, her face twisted into anguish. "I'm sorry. You're right. I didn't mean to lash out at you. You're only here to protect me. I just feel like the walls are closing in around me."

He approached and took her in his arms then. Sierra hugged him back, her face pressed against his shoulder. Bryce wanted to comfort her, but old feelings for her were stirring so easily the more time he spent with her.

*Lord, how do I protect my heart?* She'd hurt him once. He'd come here only as a friend, and didn't want to get hurt like that again. But it was becoming increasingly clear that the struggle with his feelings for her was far from over.

Sierra stepped away. "Well, at least this gives us more time to search for Raul. If I'm only working at the store part-time and then have nothing else to do, I have more time to fight to get my life of peace and quiet back."

In her eyes he saw that she wanted that more than anything. Terror was quickly beginning to reign in her life again.

Bryce frowned. Sure they'd discussed going out there and searching for Raul, but he was sure that wasn't what the sheriff had in mind when he'd taken her off deputy duties. In fact, Bryce imagined that what the sheriff had in mind for her was stay inside and wait for others to track Raul down—the exact opposite of what she was planning to do with her new freedom.

Now Bryce's job would be even more difficult.

The perfect distraction came later that day when a SAR call came in. A couple of snowshoers hadn't returned. Sierra had driven the mountain roads and finally parked at the trailhead. The volunteer searchers would follow, but Samson needed time to search the area without other people confusing the scents.

She hopped from the vehicle and opened the door for Samson to jump out. She kept him leashed for the moment. She was dressed in the typical search-and-rescue gear, along with a bright orange jacket over a Kevlar vest per Sheriff's request. Sierra studied Bryce, who had come along with her. She couldn't shake him so easily, for which she was secretly grateful.

He'd donned his own vest too, just in case. They looked like they were going on a raid rather than searching for people lost in the wilderness.

"This feels so over-the-top," she said.

"You really think so? It seems sensible to

me. You're not going out without protection, especially with a target on your back."

She got out the snowshoes and they each donned a pair. She preferred snowshoes to a snowmobile because clues could be missed as she searched.

She squatted next to Samson to release the leash. Looking into his eyes, she rubbed his ears. They'd been together and trained together. She knew his signals, and he understood her, as well.

Now… *"Zooch!"* Find. "Go find people."

Samson barked and took off, running through the snow.

"Wait," Bryce said. "What are you doing?"

Sierra angled her head at him. "We're in the wilderness. Samson is searching for people. He's following the smells in the air to find them. He's cross-trained for trailing which can include tracking from an article, but dogs are smart and finding someone can include tracking via the ground or the air. He's certified in avalanche searches, as well." She took off after Samson as quickly as she could in snowshoes. "So we're doing an area search now based on the scent. But he can air scent for humans without an article or an initial scent to go from." She scratched her head. "I'm sorry—you probably know all that stuff."

Bryce had gotten her the dog, but he hadn't gone through the K-9 training himself. Still, she hadn't wanted to insult him.

"Not at all. You sound like an expert to me." He huffed a laugh. "I always knew he was a good dog, but that's impressive."

Sierra hiked along the mountain trail alongside Bryce, her self-imposed bodyguard. "So here we are. This is the high probability area where the subjects supposedly left to hike. Samson knows to find a human scent and then search."

"What if he finds the wrong person?"

"That can happen in a search like this. If it does, we tell him he's a good dog and then to find again. And we just keep looking."

"And he won't track the others searching?"

"Not yet. They're coming in behind us. That's why we go in first."

"What happens next?"

"We'll give him time to explore and he should alert me soon if he finds anything." They walked a bit farther, and Sierra couldn't help smiling. "I love the switch to wilderness from the city—it's refreshing in ways you can't imagine. Though of course it's challenging too. There was no question we would train for avalanches."

"Again, impressive."

She shrugged.

"How often do you train?"

"I like to train with him every day, but the last few days we've gotten off our schedule. We meet with others every other week and train together."

Bryce glanced at her intermittently while he hiked across the top of the snow. "This suits you."

Admiration clung to his silver-blue gaze and her heart tripped up. She stumbled forward then righted herself on her snowshoes.

"Careful there."

"I'm fine." She was the expert hiker here, but it didn't look like it.

*Get a grip, Sierra. You can't fall for him.* Time to redirect. "You said this suits me."

She wasn't sure she completely understood what he'd meant.

"Being here in the small town where you grew up. The mountains right at your back door sans the smog. And the dog." An emotion beyond mere admiration surfaced in his eyes.

Sierra wanted to pull her gaze away from his but she couldn't.

Samson's deep throaty bark startled her and broke the moment. She jerked around to search the woods. Through the trees she could

Elizabeth Goddard 111

see her big dog plowing his way through the snow toward them.

She worked hard with him all the time and could read him. As soon as she acknowledged him he turned around—his way of alerting her that he would lead her. He'd found someone.

Sierra radioed the sheriff. "We can't know if it's them. I'll let you know as soon as we're there."

Through the woods, she could see other searchers.

Samson barked and tirelessly tilled through the snow.

"Oh, no…"

"What is it?" Bryce asked.

"Up ahead, see? It looks like… It looks like there was an avalanche." She picked up her pace and radioed the sheriff again to let him know.

"Well Samson can find them, then. You said he was an avalanche dog now."

"If they were buried in that, they're dead by now."

Sorrow infused her but she pushed it away as she caught up to Samson who had his nose to the ground, sniffing at the snow that recently collapsed from the mountain face looming above them.

His actions let her know that he might have

found someone. Saint Bernard dogs were one of the preferred breeds for avalanche dogs, and they were descended from mastiffs. Still, she didn't doubt that no matter the task, Samson was the dog to get it done. He was faithful, hardworking and enthusiastic. Her heart warmed with love for him.

On top of the snow, Samson whined but seemed confused, then, with his nose in the air, he suddenly took off again and disappeared into the woods.

"I don't understand," Bryce said.

"Neither do I, but let's go."

A shout resounded.

Bryce grabbed her arm. "Wait, Sierra. I have a bad feeling about this."

She yanked her arm free. "Samson is barking. He found someone. It could be the hikers we're searching for."

"Over here!" a woman called. "Please help us!"

Sierra spotted someone in the shadows under the overhang of a rocky ledge. She hiked toward the area and, as she got closer, two people could be seen in the shadows. Sierra's heart rate jumped. Could it be the snowshoers?

She tried to pick up the pace, but moving quickly was difficult in snowshoes. Already she was gasping for breath. Finally she approached the woman on the ground. A man was sprawled out, but his head rested on her lap.

"Are you McKayla Markum? McKayla and Jim?"

"Yes." McKayla choked out the words. "I'm so glad you found us. Please help. My husband's been shot. I've put pressure on the wound, but—" Tears overcame her.

Samson sat close to the woman, panting and whining. He pawed the snow. Sierra took that to mean he was concerned too.

Sierra called the sheriff to let the others know that Samson had found the missing snowshoers and that medical assistance was required. A gunshot wound was a serious injury. Since he was not instantly killed, the greatest danger was that he could bleed out. If he was still alive, McKayla had done a good job of slowing the bleeding, and the cold could have helped too. But the temperature presented other complications since hypothermia would also be an issue.

"Help is on the way." Sierra dropped to her knees. The snow was packed where McKayla and Jim had been waiting. "What happened?"

Tears streaked McKayla's face. "An avalanche almost took us out. We made it out of the way, but then we came across someone.

He acted like he was here to help us, but I…" Her teeth chattered making it difficult to understand her. "He wanted to hurt us. I don't know why. My husband fought him but was shot. Still, I got the weapon when the guy dropped it." Her hands shook and she pressed it over a gun next to her. "I would have used it, but he ran off. And I couldn't shoot him in the back no matter that he attacked us. I couldn't do it."

Fear corded Sierra's throat. "What did he look like?"

"His face was mostly covered, you know, with a cap, and sunglasses. He seemed tall and bulky. It's hard to tell with winter clothes and coats, but he seemed large. Jim tried to protect me." McKayla couldn't finish. She pressed her faced against her unconscious husband's forehead.

Sierra shared a glance with Bryce. An escaped convict was in the region. Was the man who attacked the Markums Raul Novack? If so, maybe he thought they'd recognized him and he hadn't wanted anyone to report his whereabouts. But his actions were counterintuitive.

Samson growled and paced. Bryce grabbed Sierra and forced her to look at him. "Raul could still be here which means you're in danger.

Now's your chance to let Samson do what he does best. He can track a criminal. Raul is hurting others, Sierra. We have to stop him now."

Sierra looked closely at where McKayla still pressed her hands against Jim's wound in the side of his gut. "You can let go. I'll take over now. You must be tired. I'll keep the pressure on. Help is coming."

McKayla appeared slightly relieved, though deep lines of worry were carved into her thirty-something face. She was scared for Jim. "I… My cell… I couldn't get a signal to call for help."

"Give him the command." Bryce pleaded with Sierra.

"No. We'd send him to his death. Besides we have to stay here with McKayla."

*Come on, Sheriff Locke! Come on, medical assistance.*

She continued to press her hand against the blood-soaked scarves McKayla had used against the wound. "We don't know if this was Raul's doing."

"Don't we?"

"I'm not sure if Samson can even detect the scent from a gun that has had so many hands on it."

"You don't need that, remember? He can air scent. He can find anyone. We know the man who shot Jim ran that way, though the tracks are gone now."

Sierra had noticed that too. McKayla and Jim had done well to find a place to keep out of the falling snow.

"May I?" She eyed the gun.

McKayla handed it over.

"No, just set it down there in front of the dog."

"Samson." Sierra forced the right voice and tone to come out. *"Verloren!"* Find whoever belongs to the gun.

The massive beast took off as if he'd been waiting for the chance.

Bryce started after Samson.

Sierra glared at Bryce. "I'm coming too!"

"No. Someone has to stay with McKayla, until help arrives."

She eyed the search and rescue volunteers, who'd left their snowmobiles behind in rough terrain and hiked toward them. Help was arriving soon.

Then she was going after Bryce and Samson.

# EIGHT

Bryce followed Samson's tracks, huffing and puffing. If he was made to do this with any regularity, he'd have to train on snowshoes to get in the right kind of shape. The scent of evergreens filled his nose. His snowshoes crunched on the snow, the only sound in the quiet, white-blanketed wilderness.

He hadn't caught sight of Samson or Raul yet. But he watched and listened as he hiked and tried to catch up.

In the distance a vicious bark resounded. Deep and throaty—it must be Samson. Bryce hadn't heard that degree of hostility from the dog before, even when they'd taken gunfire. Adrenaline pumped through him.

Samson must have found his target.

A man shouted, the sound coming from the same direction as Samson's bark. Bryce was torn—if it was Raul, everything in him screamed he should tell Samson to attack.

But he couldn't know for sure. Still, if it was the man who'd shot Jim then he needed to be detained.

What was that word in German? Samson might not listen to Bryce's command, but it was worth a try.

"Attack! *Fassen!*"

Samson wouldn't simply attack unless he sensed the man was a threat.

Gunfire resounded...

Bryce's gut tensed.

*Oh, Samson... Oh, no...*

He couldn't catch his breath but forced himself to keep moving forward. "Samson! Come on, boy. Come here." What word had she used to call Samson back to her again?

Suddenly Sierra was behind him, and almost on him. That startled him. She'd caught up? Apparently, she was more accustomed to hiking in this wilderness.

"Samson. *Heir!*" She shouted for Samson. "I don't like this," she said to Bryce. "I can't see a thing."

Bryce couldn't see through the dense trees, nor could he hear Samson barking. Dread rose in his chest. They followed the tracks.

Sierra left Bryce behind and jogged on her snowshoes. "Sierra, wait. You could be putting yourself in danger. Wait for me."

But she didn't listen. He caught up to her through a copse of trees that opened up to a clearing. Samson was there, licking at his fur. Crimson spread on the white snow.

Sierra grabbed his head. "Good boy. It's going to be okay."

Bryce caught up to them. "What is it?"

"A gunshot wound." She glared at Bryce. Then tried to look at the wound but Samson nipped at her. "Shh, it's okay, boy. I need to help. Let me look, okay?" She shook her head. "I can't see. But I need to stop the bleeding."

Like McKayla had used her scarf on Jim, Sierra tugged her scarf off and folded it. She pressed it gently against Samson's fur, he growled and placed his massive maw over her hand, but didn't bite.

Sierra obviously trusted him not to lash out, but Bryce wouldn't trust any dog that much. Sierra got on her radio to let the search team know that Samson needed medical help too.

Bryce let his gaze roam the woods. "Whoever shot Samson is still out there, Sierra." *Raul is still out there.* "I thought McKayla said she got his gun, but apparently he had more than one."

"One that he couldn't get to without her

shooting him, so he fled," she said. "But he could have killed Samson with one shot."

He felt her eyes boring into him so he finally looked back at her. "You're wondering why he didn't."

She nodded.

"He could have stumbled and missed. Maybe he wasn't really aiming—he could have shot at Samson and kept running, not realizing he hadn't killed Samson. We can't know. If Samson hadn't been shot, he could have brought Raul down."

Her frowned deepened. "Whatever. Samson could be down-and-out now for SAR. Other tracking dogs were brought in and haven't found Raul yet. But our team has spotted him now so maybe they'll scour this region and find him soon."

The sheriff had told Bryce the state had set up a command center at a ranger station outside of town so they wouldn't disrupt the ice festival. So far he and Sierra hadn't seen or heard the dogs looking for Raul, except for a couple in town. The bulk of the dogs were in the woods and up in the mountains far from where Sierra and Bryce were now. The terrain was treacherous and the region vast—even with dogs, it seemed impossible to search it all.

Samson whined and licked at his wound. "Come on buddy, you're okay," she said.

"Maybe it's just a graze."

He wished he hadn't said the words. She pulled first aid from her backpack. "I'll see if he'll let me take a look."

Samson had finally calmed though he still whined. He lay across the snow, but remained alert. Sierra removed her bloodied scarf. "I think the bleeding is slowing." She peered at the wound without touching it. "I'm no expert, but it doesn't look like an actual hole in his body it… It's more like a slice over his skin. Do you think Raul cut him with a knife and this wasn't a gunshot wound?"

"I heard the gunfire."

Sierra gently placed gauze over the wound then taped it. It wouldn't stick well or hold tight on Samson's fur. "The vet will have to shave his fur. But—" she hung her head "—this could have been so much worse."

Right. The dog could have died. Guilt flooded Bryce—he understood Sierra's reservations much better now, though he'd known the danger all along.

"And it could still be that much worse. I think we need to get out of here. We're too exposed here in these woods."

"Okay, Samson. We need to try to walk back to the others."

"Come on, boy." She leashed Samson. He growled and barked, but got to his feet.

"Get down!" Bryce covered Sierra.

She kept a hold of the leash. "Get off me, Bryce."

"He's still here. Samson was warning us."

Gunfire rang out again. A bullet slammed into a nearby tree, shattering bark. Bryce covered her again.

"We need backup. Someone to help us here, and soon. Definitely not volunteers. Radio your sheriff to let him know."

Shouts rang out from the direction they'd come, along with more gunfire.

Sierra got on her radio to relay about the shooter. "Searchers are out here and this could be dangerous for them. Most of them are volunteers!"

Sierra shrugged away from Bryce's protection and brandished her own weapon. "The other deputies won't get here in time. This is up to us. You and me. Let's get him."

She started to rise and he pulled her down, keeping his grip on her this time and refusing to release her despite her protests.

Sierra stared at him, fury pouring from her gaze. "You agreed to help me find him."

"Not like this," Bryce said. "He has the advantage. He can see us but we can't see him. Besides, you haven't forgotten Samson, have you? He needs medical attention."

Samson panted, drool hanging from both sides of his mouth. At the mention off his name, he licked Bryce.

"I want to go after him too," he said. "But not like this." Not with Samson compromised. "There'll be another chance and we'll have the advantage." He was making promises he couldn't keep.

A deputy rushed forward. "Sheriff said you should be safe now."

"Wait." Sierra shared a look at Bryce. "What? How can I be safe? Did he get Raul?"

"We saw him crossing a river on our approach up the trail. So went after him. Then we lost him. The terrain was too rocky. We'll bring the dogs to this area today to search." The deputy frowned. "I see Samson is hurt."

"Yes. He's going to be okay though. Aren't you, boy?"

"We need law enforcement who climb too," the deputy continued. "The way he disappeared, he looks to be great at rock climbing."

Bryce frowned. "This time of year it's more like ice—"

"Climbing," Sierra said. "Ice climbing."

Samson whined as if in pain. Sierra reassured the dog, who had warned her and tried to protect her. The dog's injury was on Bryce, and Sierra would probably not let him forget it.

Back in the Jeep with Samson, Bryce drove this time so Sierra could sit in the back holding the dog. He steered back to town, following the directions she gave him for the office of the local vet. "Raul couldn't possibly be here for the ice climbing festival," he said. "That would just… That wouldn't make any sense."

"No, it wouldn't. I think he somehow got away. He's eluded the search dogs because he somehow knows his way around this terrain and he can go places they can't go. But that's just an assumption on my part," she said.

"But Samson knows his way around too, right?" Bryce glanced in the rearview mirror to get a glimpse of Sierra and her dog.

"I don't want to put him out there again before he's ready."

"Let's hope his wound is truly only superficial and will heal quickly."

"I hope that too, but he could have died today, Bryce."

*Oh, Sierra.*

The vet, after a long visit, patched Samson up and gave him an otherwise clean bill of health, commenting that after a day or two Samson would be as good as new. But to be certain—mostly to appease Sierra's concern—he would keep the dog with him overnight.

Bryce parked the Jeep around the side of the building and escorted her back to the toy store that had closed an hour ago. He'd had to drive around a few times to get that parking spot as the town had started to fill up with those coming to view the big competitions this weekend.

Sierra walked through the toy store to the back and then unlocked and opened up the apartment. "Dad?" she said as she stepped inside.

Then she looked around, and screamed.

The apartment had been sacked.

She pressed her hand over her mouth. "Dad!"

Sierra sprinted up the stairs and was practically yanked down as Bryce tugged her behind him. "Call the sheriff for backup."

"You're not—" She didn't bother finishing.

Bryce had already drawn his gun. "I'm getting you out of here."

"Not without my father you aren't."

"You don't know that he's here."

She brandished her own gun. Determination drove her to push past Bryce. "But I'll know soon enough."

"Then let's get to it, but I'm going in first." He started up the stairs.

Sierra called dispatch as they climbed the steps. She understood that Bryce trusted her as a deputy, but right now he was trying to protect her from Raul, and that changed the dynamics.

"John, are you here?" Bryce shouted the question.

At this point, they weren't trying to surprise whoever had broken into the home. But Bryce still wanted to use himself as a shield for Sierra.

"Dad!" she shouted.

She had never fully been able to be rid of Raul and now it was as though he had stepped right out of her nightmares. Fear for her father nearly paralyzed her but she and Bryce managed to clear the two rooms upstairs.

Catching her breath to slow her pounding heart, she leaned against the hallway wall. "If he's not here, then where is he?" She looked at her cell. "He didn't leave any texts to tell me where he is, but I'm texting him now. Then I'll call too for good measure."

Somewhere downstairs, shouts resounded.

"Must be backup," Bryce said. "Up here!"

Bryce put his gun away and leaned in close to look her in the eyes. "Sierra, you okay?"

"No. Not until I find Dad. You don't think—" Could Raul have taken him? *Oh, no. No, no, no.* Her legs grew weak and she leaned against the wall with her cell to her ear, praying Dad would answer her call.

Sheriff Locke climbed the steps. "Got your emergency call. I just returned from taking the statement of the two snowshoers. Looks like someone has done a number—"

"Sheriff," she interrupted. "My dad. He's not here."

Deputy Colfax stepped up next to the sheriff. "John's at the café across the street. I just left there when I got the call to come here. So far, it doesn't look like he knows there's any trouble."

"Oh." She pressed her hand against her chest and relief whooshed through her. "I was so worried. I thought—I thought something happened to him."

Or that Raul had taken him.

And why hadn't he answered her text or call?

"Jane!" She called her friend and employee

on her cell. "We need to make sure she wasn't hurt," she said to Bryce.

Jane answered right away. "Sierra! Hey. What's up? Don't tell me I forgot to turn the lights off again."

Sierra eyed the men watching her. "No, nothing like that. I'm just glad to hear that you're okay. Where are you?"

"I'm at home getting ready for a dinner date tonight."

"Oh good. Is it with that Chuck guy?"

"I'm so over him. No. His name is Chris."

"Okay, well please be careful. Someone broke into the apartment and ransacked it. As far as I can tell they didn't touch the store."

Jane gasped. "Oh, no. You're kidding! This must have something to do with the man after you." Sierra had told Jane some of what was going on, and to let her know if she saw anyone suspicious in the store.

"One would assume that's exactly who's responsible."

"What do you think he was looking for?"

"I have no idea." Sierra eased down the stairs and looked around the apartment. The coffee table in the living room had been overturned. Chairs too. Books pulled from the shelves. And the kitchen... Her stomach soured. She drew in a breath. "I just wanted to make sure that you're all right. Please be careful."

"Why are you telling me this? You don't think I'm a target do you?"

"No. I just think it's common sense."

Jane chuckled though she didn't sound convinced. "All right then. Unless there's anything else, I need to get going."

"I do too. Text me when you get home safe and sound after your date, okay? I'll see you tomorrow."

Sierra ended the call. The sheriff, Deputy Colfax and Bryce all stared at her as if waiting to hear about Jane.

"I guess you heard she's safe," she said. "Which means that whoever broke in must have done so after Jane left, unless they came through the back. Working up front, she might not have noticed or heard anything coming from the apartment." Sierra hugged herself. "I need to talk to Dad."

"Miguel is with him now, escorting him over," Deputy Colfax said. "They should be here any second."

"We don't want to contaminate the scene," Sheriff Locke said. "But he needs to see this. Maybe he will see something missing, who knows."

"Does he know what happened yet?" she asked.

"Only that someone broke in and you're all right," the sheriff said. "Can you tell us if you've noticed anything missing? Though my gut tells me this wasn't a burglary."

"Exactly. We know who did this."

Deputy Colfax scratched his head. "I'm not so sure."

"What do you mean?" Bryce asked.

"Why would Raul ransack your home? He's after *you*, remember?"

"I think he's trying to shake Sierra up," Bryce said. "Intimidate her with fear tactics."

"If that was him out there today who attacked those two hikers, he's mixing up his tactics."

"That could have been a simple matter of him getting you out there with Samson to search for missing people. But his plans to hurt you didn't work out." Sheriff Locke rubbed his chin. "I hate to pull you from SAR too."

"Sheriff, please don't."

"He's right, Sierra." Bryce crossed his arms. "If Raul thinks you'll be out there with Samson searching for someone lost in the wilderness, he could try that tactic again. That puts others at risk."

She blew out a defeated breath. She hadn't thought about it like that. Raul was shutting her world down.

"Okay. Okay. I get it. But it doesn't look like staying home would keep me safe either. As far as him breaking into my apartment, he could do it again," she said. "Next time Dad might not be so fortunate as to be somewhere else."

"Which brings me to another point," Bryce said. "We need to figure out how someone got in and make sure that can never happen again."

Bryce kept fisting his hands. She understood his frustration and feelings of helplessness.

"I should get busy and see if there's something missing." She knew there wouldn't be, but this was all part of the investigative process.

Sierra glanced through Dad's room and as she suspected, found nothing missing—but what a mess. They all suspected Raul had done this when she and Bryce had gone to the vet. He'd come off that mountain and headed straight for her home to do this. To torture her. He was a sick, sick man.

She hated being in his sights. Exhaustion

and wariness already ate at the edges of her composure as she moved to her own room.

She and Bryce had already cleared the room so she'd seen the mess, but she feared what she might find there upon closer examination.

A shiver crept up her spine. She'd been sleeping in this bed, this room last night and she'd had nightmares about Raul. It felt like he'd stepped from those nightmares right into her room.

*He was here in my room.*

She rubbed at the goose bumps, but they remained.

*God, how do I get him out of my life? When will this end? I don't understand why it's happening.*

She wiped tears from her cheeks, then moved to head out of the room.

A small slip of paper next to the bed caught her attention. She picked it up, then read the words.

*"I'm going to finish what I started that night four years ago."*

Her hands shook. The trembling took over her entire body. She couldn't show this to Dad.

"Sierra, what is it?"

Bryce rushed forward. She glanced up at him. "This. He left me a note."

Concern poured from his gaze, then he looked over her shoulder to read the note before taking it and laying it on the side table. Bryce turned her to face him. She looked into his eyes where emotion and concern for her trumped anything he might have said, and then simply pulled her into his arms.

Comfort seemed to exude from his every fiber and she soaked it up, but she knew that he was restraining his anger. Not at her, but at the circumstances. She understood he felt powerless to stop the events from unfolding. What could possibly happen next?

Finally she stepped away from him. She hadn't wanted to need him, but Bryce had been here for her just as he had that night when Raul attacked her. "It's like we've come full circle."

"We won't let this happen again."

Bold words. Sierra was unsure what more they could do to prevent it except call in the National Guard to surround her everywhere she went. "Please don't tell Dad about the note. I don't want him more upset than he already is. I'm going to distract him and you can show it to Sheriff Locke. Okay?"

Bryce nodded. She wasn't sure she could

express to him how much she appreciated his support. But she thought he probably already understood.

She was on her way down the steps when Dad appeared at the bottom.

"Oh, Dad." She bounded the rest of the way down and hugged him on the last step.

She thought he would never let her go— and that was just fine with her. She'd been so afraid that she'd lost him. That Raul had killed him or taken him to get to her. "Somehow, this has got to end."

He released her then peered at her, overwhelming concern in his eyes. "How's Samson?"

His question surprised her. "He's going to be all right. The vet wanted to keep him overnight to be sure."

"I'd prefer it if he were here to protect you."

Now she understood why he'd jumped right to that.

Sheriff Locke approached. "The state's coming in to process the scene. See if they can get some fingerprints. We don't have the resources for that, so they'll take care of it."

Sierra stared at him. "So you're saying we can't sleep here."

He shook his head. "I'd give their evidence processing team a couple of days to get here and get it done, then you can come home again. The store wasn't disturbed, so you're good to keep that open."

"You've got to be kidding." Sierra scraped both hands through her hair and hung her head back. But then again, did she really want to sleep in that room where Raul had been mere hours ago, after eluding them up where the snowshoers had run into him?

Sheriff Locke moved away as he got a call on his cell.

"Bryce, what was he doing up in the mountains?" she asked. If he had been hiding somewhere up in that area, the searchers would have come across his hiding spot, and he would have to move.

"Maybe that's what Raul wanted," Bryce said. "To get you out of this apartment so he could take a shot at you, only he missed. He injured Samson, knowing you'd be at the vet, and came here to leave you that note. He loves this game of terror."

Sheriff Locke finished the call then approached Sierra.

"Sierra, you and John are welcome to stay at my place," Sheriff Locke said. "Barbara would be happy for the company."

Barbara was her boss's wife.

"Oh, no, I couldn't impose."

"The biggest event of the festival is tomorrow. You're not going to get a room at a hotel tonight," Sheriff Locke said. "Give me a yes and I'll let Barbara know. Bryce, I'll add you in to the count, and don't say you couldn't impose. Your protective services are required so I insist."

Bryce nodded. "I won't give up my hotel room, though, so I'll have a place to stay in a couple of days."

"Fair enough. Everything should be back to normal in a day or two. Who knows, maybe we'll have tracked Raul down and caught him by then."

One thing Sierra knew: she would have to come to terms with the fact that Raul had chosen to come into her room. He'd let her know that he could get to her whenever he wanted. He'd chosen not to kill Samson but had harmed him enough that she would spend hours at the vet, showing that he could also get to her dog if he wanted. He could hurt her in so many ways, whenever he chose.

And he would choose the time and place to end her life.

And…she had to come to terms with the fact that the whole reason Bryce had gifted her with the English mastiff puppy was for protection. Sierra had fallen in love with that dog and removed him from that role—to a point. Sure he could warn her of danger here at home, but she didn't want him to face off against a criminal holding a deadly weapon.

In her current situation, with a killer after her, how did she prevent that from happening again?

# NINE

In his Subaru Forester, Bryce had followed the sheriff to what he'd been told would be a sprawling log cabin with a wraparound porch situated somewhere just outside of Crescent Springs. Sierra and John had ridden with the sheriff along with Samson. Sierra had been too worried that Raul would somehow try to get to the dog at the veterinarian hospital, so she'd gotten him released. The vet had agreed that Sierra could take her dog with her and that she would call him tonight if she noticed anything concerning.

Sierra had told Bryce all about the sheriff's dogs, Turner and Hooch, from the Tom Hanks movie by the same name, though these dogs weren't big dogs, but corgis. Somehow that totally didn't fit what Bryce would expect to see from the sheriff. But he understood better after learning the dogs mostly belonged to the sheriff's wife, Barbara. Turner and

Hooch weren't K-9 or SAR dogs but were purely spoiled pets.

Sierra had mentioned her concern about bringing Samson with them to Sheriff Locke's place. Samson needed to take it easy and not get caught up in playing with Turner and Hooch, but the sheriff's wife had promised to make her pets behave.

So for a night or two they were going to be one big happy family.

He thought back to the whole family thing. He'd once thought that he wanted exactly that, and he'd allowed his heart to take that risk in caring deeply, loving someone, hoping for a future.

First with Rebecca.

He'd let himself, no holds barred, fall head over heels for her, and had been foolish enough to believe she had fallen in love with him in return. He thought back to that moment that he'd planned to propose. He'd planned to meet her at a nice restaurant. He'd walked in with a little black velvet box in his pocket. They'd enjoyed a nice dinner and as his hopes had risen and his palms slicked for that moment that would soon be upon them, ushered in with dessert, Rebecca had proceeded to explain how much and how deeply she cared about Bryce…but that she had met someone else. This other man, she explained, was a better fit for her because Rebecca hadn't wanted to grow too serious with a police officer.

Really? She could have said no to that first date then.

He followed the sheriff who turned down a winding drive. Bryce had gotten over Rebecca. Learned his lesson and his heart had grown a little bit harder. Then he'd met Sierra—a woman who was in law enforcement too, who understood the risks involved and wouldn't judge him for them. They'd connected in a way he could never connect with anyone else, especially considering their battle with the Novack brothers.

Bryce had... He'd loved Sierra. But he knew to take it slowly and not confess those feelings or consider proposing until he knew she felt the same. He had believed she was beginning to return his love.

So, yes, Bryce had been foolish again and let himself fall.

But after Raul had attacked her, Sierra had cut ties with Bryce. She didn't want to care too deeply, she'd said. He had known about her past and that she'd loved a highway patrolman who had been shot and killed on duty. Raul nearly killing Bryce had brought that back for her.

So with Bryce's track record, a relationship with Sierra, any relationship, seemed like it wasn't worth the risk. A happy family was a pipe dream.

He still cared about Sierra and was here for her now to see that she made it through this alive.

The sheriff finally parked his vehicle and out climbed the happy gang. Bryce exited his own vehicle and yanked his small duffel from the seat.

A slender brunette stood in the doorway of the cabin and let the corgis run out, barking and wagging their tails. Turner and Hooch.

Samson's deep bark mixed with their yaps.

Yep. One big happy family.

Bryce pulled his gaze from the joy and took in the surrounding woods. So the sheriff thought this would be a good idea. No wonder he'd made sure Bryce came along for the ride and stayed too. After he met the wife and dogs and settled in, he'd make sure to check the perimeter. This wouldn't be a vacation.

He never imagined it would be.

Not until Raul was out of their lives for good. Not until Sierra was safe.

Then Bryce would go back to his life in Boulder.

* * *

Samson snored loudly at her feet.

Turner and Hooch had been put to bed like young children. They slept in Barbara's room.

Sierra yawned, wishing she was already sleeping in the guest room offered by Sheriff Locke and the hospitable Barbara. Dad had long ago gone to sleep in one of the extra rooms. The day had been long and terrifying on so many fronts that it had left her exhausted. But instead of resting, hoping she could sleep without nightmares or fears of Raul preventing her, she sat on the comfy sofa across from Barbara, sipping the hot cocoa her hostess had offered. Bryce and the sheriff were outside making sure no one was stalking the house.

Neither of them believed Raul would find her here or dare to attack her while she was at the sheriff's house, but just in case, the state had loaned Officer Kendall to them for night duty, and the sheriff and Bryce were giving the area another once-over. The sheriff's home had become an unintended safe house—except that her whereabouts weren't exactly a secret.

"Thanks for letting us impose on you for a night or two, Barbara." Sierra watched her over the brim of her cup.

Barbara was about a decade younger than the sheriff's late forties, and she was a talented artist—her paintings and decor brightened the walls. She offered a soft smile. "We're more than happy to open up our home. We don't get guests nearly enough and, without kids, we can't expect grandkids in our future."

Sierra resisted the urge to suggest Barbara get a SAR dog and get involved in that kind of work. That would be so worthwhile, but Barbara spoke first.

"The way you and Bryce look at each other, one could almost construe something was going on. I see by that flash in your eyes that *was* is the operative word."

Sierra measured her next words, then asked, "Do all artists read people so well?"

Barbara laughed, clearly pleased to learn she'd hit her mark. "Some do. But with you and Bryce, I think anyone could see that there's something more going on."

"*Was* going on. Yes, we saw each other when we both lived in Boulder."

"The way you look at each other begs the question—what happened? Surely you could work out whatever it was that broke you two up."

Sierra stared at the fire, exhaustion flooding her. Did she want to open up all of it to Barbara? She'd moved back to Crescent Springs wanting to escape and she'd done well for a year. But the least she could do was answer this sweet woman's question.

"Before Bryce, there was someone else." Sierra frowned at the thought.

"Oh, honey. I'm sorry if I overstepped. You don't have to tell me."

She was already in so she would finish. "No, it's okay. I thought I was in love. No, wait. I *was* in love with a guy named Buck Thomas. He was Colorado Highway Patrol. One day he stopped a driver whose taillight was out—a simple traffic stop. Oddly enough those simple stops are one of the most productive ways of catching the bad guys. The next thing you know, he was shot and killed. I don't think Buck knew what hit him. But I do. He'd pulled over someone who was transporting drugs. They thought it was worth it to kill him to try to evade justice."

"I'm so sorry."

"It's been five years and time heals most wounds. I told myself I wouldn't care about anyone in law enforcement again. Then I met Bryce. He got under my skin before I knew what was happening and I became close to him. But…"

"What happened?"

Sierra hadn't meant to get this detailed. "Raul happened. He nearly killed us both. I knew then I needed to distance myself from Bryce. I couldn't bear it if he got hurt again because of me. I couldn't go through someone else I cared about getting killed. Someone I loved. Unfortunately, I also love my dog. Bryce gave him to me. I trained him for protection and to search for and detain those the police were after. But then a friend's K-9 was killed in the line of fire and that's when I decided I'd had enough. I couldn't let Samson die too, so I moved here. I cross-trained him for wilderness search and rescue and avalanche searches, so here we are."

"Yes." Barbara gazed into the fire too, as if lost in thought. "And Bryce is here too. Looks like you can't get away from those who care about you even if you try."

Barbara offered Sierra a soft smile, then she rose from the chair. Squeezing Sierra's shoulder as she moved past, she said, "I'm going to leave you to your thoughts and do a few chores before bed. Feel free to turn in if you want. Oh, and I see Bryce is already back."

He stepped all the way into the room from the hallway. Had he come in the back door? "The sheriff is in the mudroom cleaning up."

Sierra risked a glance his way and found Bryce studying her as though he had heard every word she'd said about him.

Oh, no.

# TEN

Bryce edged closer to the sofa opposite Sierra, uncertain if she wanted his company.

Chewing her bottom lip, she watched him approach—with that look in her eyes. It was obvious that she wondered if he'd heard what she'd said to Barbara.

Should he tell her? Or spare her the pain? He'd come in through the back and padded down the hallways in his socks. Sheriff Locke had remained outside talking to Officer Kendall.

When Bryce had heard her voice and mention of Buck, he'd paused. He should have made himself known or headed the other way so he wouldn't eavesdrop, but his feet became cemented in the floor.

He didn't think he could bear the discussion of their past loves and their breakup himself, so said, "Do you ever wish you lived somewhere like Florida?"

She rewarded him with a smile and a burst of laughter. "Where did that come from?"

"Are you kidding me? It's cold out there. Brrrr." He rubbed his arms for effect.

She angled her head, her smile soft. He wished her lips didn't appear so inviting. He was positive she didn't intend that, but they did have a history, after all. He should good and well remember the other part of their history and why he was here at this moment.

Stay focused on protecting her.

"I guess I've never thought about it," she said. "Growing up in the mountains, I couldn't see living anywhere else. Maybe Florida or some warm beach with palm trees would be a nice break and make me appreciate my home even more. But I can't think that far into the future at the moment."

He heard in her tone what she hadn't said—Raul was consuming all her attention.

"Uh… Bryce?"

Uh. Oh. "Yeah?"

"I've been thinking."

He leaned forward until his elbows were on his thighs. "I'm not sure that's such a good thing."

She threw a pillow at him and he caught it. "Hey."

"Hey, yourself."

"So what have you been thinking?" He rubbed his chin. This was going to be a long night on multiple fronts.

"You and I discussed going out there and searching for Raul ourselves. Samson and I know the area better than the state police and their dogs. We could come across an obscure place—a cabin or a mine—out of sight. Some place he could be hiding out. It's far better than waiting around here for him to come and get me. That he's crazy is obvious, but—" she shivered, even sitting close to a crackling fire "—being targeted and obsessed over by a sick person like him is unnerving in a thousand ways. We have to get him before he gets us. We have to find him."

"But you don't want to take Samson out there until he's ready for that." And that was only if she would allow Samson to search for Raul, at all, especially after what happened today. But he wouldn't bring it up.

"Exactly where I was going with this. To-morrow is the mixed climbing, one of the main competitions in the festival, so it's going to be über-crowded. Raul knows his way around. He must have some skills in mountain climbing. Maybe ice climbing, like we discussed. We should go to the event and see if he makes an appearance. He'll think he can hide in the crowd."

"I don't know, Sierra. Your safety is the most important thing." Should he tell her? "Tonight when we checked the perimeter, the sheriff and I discussed you potentially staying here through this—as a sort of safe house."

"Dad and I are here only until the state has processed the crime scene and released our apartment. I can't stay here beyond then, Bryce. I've already texted Jane to let her know that Dad and I will be back in town in the morning in time to attend the ice climbing festivities and watch the main event with you tomorrow."

"So you won't stay here even for your dad?"

"That's a low blow and you know it."

"It's like you're *asking* Raul to come and get you."

"Maybe I am. This time I'll be waiting." Sierra shoved from the sofa and headed toward the hall. She called over her shoulder, "Be ready early—the events start at eight." Sierra nudged a sleeping Samson with her toe. "Come on, boy. Time for bed."

She disappeared down the hallway, Samson on her heels. Bryce heard the telltale sound of her door opening and closing.

Well that settled it. She'd made up her mind and all Bryce could do was follow her to the crowded event and stand in the cold until his nose froze off. He'd grown up in Florida and he'd never quite gotten used to the cold here. Still, he'd do his best to protect her while he worked by her side to bring down Raul.

In a way they were a team again, and this time, he hoped Raul would finally get put away in a place that he could never escape—somewhere far from Colorado would be optimal.

Sheriff Locke rushed into the living area. "Bryce. Rick thought he saw movement. Could be an animal, but we're going out to investigate. Bryce, you remain on guard in the house."

"You got it." Bryce immediately got to his feet and brandished his weapon. It was going to be a long night. He moved quietly through the large home, checking all the locks on the doors and windows. He came across Sheriff Locke's master bedroom and softly knocked on the door. The sheriff had entrusted him with the inside of his home, so he wouldn't make any exceptions when it came to checking things over.

Barbara answered with a concerned frown. "Is everything all right?"

"We're not sure. Will you please make sure your windows are closed and locked?"

She opened the door wide. Folded laundry was on the bed and a television program played quietly on the wide screen. "To tell you the truth, we usually do sleep with the window cracked, even in the winter. We love to sleep with lots of covers piled high."

Barbara showed Bryce the windows—they weren't locked, but Bryce secured them. "Thanks. I'm sorry to disturb you."

"No problem," she said. "I was just getting on top of laundry."

Turner and Hooch barely lifted their heads to acknowledge his entrance as they slept on big dog pillows by the wall. She'd trained them well. He left Barbara to finish the laundry. What must it be like after a long day of police work to come home to a nice log cabin in the woods and spend the evening with the woman you loved next to a big fire? Sheriff Locke had carved out a good life for himself here, though Bryce knew it wasn't entirely without its dangers. The sheriff could be called upon any time of day or night.

Still, somehow, Bryce's bachelor lifestyle didn't measure up. He was on his own because he'd resolved he wouldn't allow himself the pain of heartache again. And yet there was heartache nonetheless. The endless pain of loneliness. He brushed off the melancholy. Now wasn't the time to think about what he could have had. What he still wanted.

Next, he knocked softly on Sierra's door. Of course she would lock the window, but Bryce hadn't expected Barbara's windows to be open either, so it was better to check every single one of them.

Sierra cracked the door and peeked out, a meager grin on her face. "What do you want?"

"I'm doing a window check. Are yours locked?"

"Well of course they're locked. Why wouldn't they... Hold on." She opened the door and then moved to the window and opened it wide, letting a cold breeze blow through. Then she closed it hard and locked it.

Sierra jerked her face to him. "Is there something going on? What's happened?"

"I don't know. Kendall thought he saw something. He and the sheriff are checking it out."

Samson was snoring per usual. He didn't seem too disturbed. "Do you think he's too drugged from whatever the vet gave him to warn you or protect you?"

Her brows pinched as she stared at him. "I'm not sure."

Sierra moved to the side table and pulled a weapon out of the drawer. "I might as well just sit in that chair with my gun all night. I'm not going to get any sleep like this."

Bryce gently took the weapon from her, surprised she so easily gave it up. He gripped her arms and peered into her eyes. "I'm here to protect you. I did it before. Please trust me to do that again for you. Tonight and for the next many days and nights until this is over." More emotion than he'd intended resounded in his words, but maybe she needed to understand the depth of his commitment.

He could see in her eyes that she wanted to trust him. He didn't miss the longing there and the images of previous kisses they'd shared crept softly across his mind and heart. That same longing coursed through every artery and vein, through his soul.

*Sierra...*

Then Bryce caught himself. Now was the absolute wrong time for this. There was a killer out there—maybe only a dozen yards away. And even if there wasn't, this moment could never happen for them.

He hitched a half grin and stepped back. "Besides, you're a mess when you go without sleep."

* * *

Sierra blinked her eyes open. *Where am I?*
The familiar rush of fear sent her heart rate into her throat, then she exhaled.

No nightmare had woken her up.

She stared at the ceiling for a moment before she got her bearings. She was in Sheriff Locke's home. And she'd fallen asleep. She'd actually slept hard. Maybe that was because Bryce had made her feel safe. That man she'd once thought she'd fallen for was here for her until this was over. She trusted him with her life, but she knew to steer clear of him in matters of the heart. She didn't trust herself when it came to her feelings for him.

But Sierra couldn't figure out why Bryce would be here for her in this way when he had his own life and business to run back in Boulder. Why would he put his life on the line for her like this? He wasn't here for some romantic dream that they might rekindle what they had been growing toward in the past. They both knew where they stood on that. She had her reasons. He had his.

They were friends, yes, or tried to be while ignoring their attraction, but Sierra hadn't realized the depth of feelings for her. Still she knew in her heart that if Bryce was in some sort of trouble she would probably rush to his aid as well—no matter the cost. Right? Friends did that for each other.

Except she'd never had that kind of friendship with anyone else. And she wasn't entirely sure hers and Bryce's relationship was completely platonic.

In fact, she needed to face and accept the truth—tonight, if he had kissed her, she would totally have let him. She had *wanted* him to kiss her, even though she'd resolved not to let herself fall for someone in his kind of career. She shouldn't live in fear, and in this way, she didn't have to. Still, if something happened to Bryce—whether she was romantically involved or not—it would crush her. He held a big place in her heart and that had never changed.

Samson drew her attention in the dim lighting. He stood by the window and a low growl rumbled in his chest.

Could that be what had woken her up?

She sat up on the edge of the bed and grabbed her weapon on the table, her breath coming fast.

That night long ago, she'd woken up to find Raul in her room. He had already taken her gun while she'd been sleeping. If he was back, he'd find that she was ready for him this time.

Sierra got up and paced the small, warmly decorated room.

The blinds were closed so it wasn't like Raul could see into the room, for which she was grateful. But Sierra really wanted to see outside. She didn't want to disturb the household if it was nothing. The sheriff and Officer Kendall had gone out checking earlier and she'd meant to wait up and see if they'd found anything. Sierra had fallen asleep.

She glanced at the clock. That had been two hours ago. So the men would have come back inside by now.

Could Samson be growling at an animal? Maybe a mountain lion was roaming around out there in freezing temperatures.

Sierra crouched to eye level with Samson and rubbed his ears. "What is it boy? Are you hungry? Thirsty? Are you in pain?"

He moved back to the window and growled, then gave a deep menacing bark.

And with that bark fear curdled in her gut.

Okay. That was it.

She backed against the wall every bit the coward she didn't want to be, hadn't expected to be, but images of Raul nearly killing her swarmed through her.

Her throat constricted until she could hardly breathe.

*He's outside the window. He's out there.*

"So get your act together and get out there and take him down." *Snap out of it.*

Sierra quickly changed into snow pants and pulled on a hoodie. In the mudroom she would grab her coat and snow boots. She would let Officer Kendall know that something might be happening.

Samson whined as she made to open the bedroom door. Even if Sierra was willing to let Samson face off against a killer, with his injury he wasn't ready. "Sorry, buddy. You need to heal."

She opened the door and found Bryce standing there as though waiting. "I heard him bark. What are you doing?"

"Raul is out there."

"How do you know?"

"I just know, okay?"

"And you're going out there to get him all by your lonesome?"

Sierra gave him an incredulous look. "Of course not. I knew you'd be standing right here. And we can get Kendall and the sheriff too. But Raul is out there. He was…" Her throat constricted again. She fought for air, then said, "I think he was at my window."

"Stay here." Bryce stomped off.

She trailed him to the mudroom. The blinds had been shut in there as well.

He found Officer Kendall putting his boots on. "It's time for my perimeter check."

"We think Raul's out there," Bryce said. "So I'm going with you."

"Notify the sheriff," Kendall said.

"Right." Bryce turned to her. "Sierra, you go let the sheriff know what's happening."

"Okay, but I'm coming with you when you head outside to search. If you leave without me, then I'll find you, so you'd better not leave."

Sierra rushed down the hallway to find the sheriff exiting his room. "We think Raul is outside."

"Because?"

How did she explain? She felt like an idiot. "It's a gut feel. Samson was growling at my window. Don't ask me how. I just… Know."

"Good enough for me. But you're staying here."

"Sheriff, I—"

"I need you to keep Barbara safe."

He left her standing there. This wasn't how she'd planned things to go down. But she couldn't leave his wife sleeping in her room—and her father, just down the hall— when Raul was outside.

Sierra stood in the hallway next to Barbara's door. Samson whined and barked from her room, wanting out. From here, she could see a portion of the mudroom and she watched the three men exit. Sierra headed that way, opening the bedroom door to let Samson come with her.

"Raul could come right through this door now that all three of them are out there, Samson. And if he does, you and I will be waiting for him."

"And me." Barbara emerged from the hallway and pumped the shotgun she held. "I'll be here waiting for him too."

Sierra couldn't help but smile, and almost wished that Raul would come through that door to face off against the three of them—Barbara, Sierra and Samson.

Barbara moved closer to the door. "I don't think it hurts to lock it though, in case he tries. We'll let the guys in when they get back."

A window shattered.

Turner and Hooch yapped, shrill and anxious, in the master bedroom.

Samson barked and ran toward the sound. Sierra commanded him to stay. Bryce's words to her about letting Samson do what he was trained to do surfaced in her mind.

*But he's a big dog. He's trained to do many things including protect. Remember you trained him to hopefully one day become part of the new BPD's K-9 unit that would work with the Boulder County Sheriff's office K-9 unit. Tonight you were afraid to let him protect you or to let him go after Raul.*

She already knew all of it, but Bryce's words stayed with her and unsettled her.

"I'll go check it out," Barbara said.

If something happened to Barbara, Sierra would never forgive herself. Samson acted as if his wound didn't affect him. She was being overly cautious.

"No. I have Samson for protection. He can also apprehend and detain a suspect. I'll take him to check it out. You stay here and watch the back door for the guys."

Barbara pursed her lips and nodded.

Sierra commanded Samson to guard. In this case he would apprehend an intruder if one existed.

*God, please keep us safe.*

He took off, an intimidating, ferocious beast of an animal.

She kept her eyes opened as she silently prayed. *Please keep Samson safe.*

Her weapon ready to aim and fire, she followed her K-9. They'd never gotten to officially work together in Boulder. How surreal this felt.

Samson sniffed at the master bedroom door and barked. Turner and Hooch continued to yap and growl, but the sounds were muted. Maybe Barbara had put them away in the bathroom to keep them out of harm's way.

Heart pounding, Sierra leaned against the wall and drew in two breaths. She prepared to come in low as she opened the door.

She flung it open, giving Samson the "attack" command. *"Fassen!"*

He dashed into the room as she aimed her weapon at empty air.

The curtain billowed with the rush of wind through the broken window. Sierra crept to the side of the window to peer out.

A shadow moved outside. "Freeze!"

"It's me, Sierra!" Bryce shouted.

She lowered the weapon and gasped. No wonder Samson hadn't jumped through the window—he'd known Bryce was there. But someone else had been there moments before.

Samson approached her. She knelt and rubbed his ears. *"Zei Brav!* Good boy."

Relief washed through her on the one hand that Samson wasn't in danger, and frustration gnawed her at the same time—how did they bring this man down?

She stood and examined the broken window. The sound of a snowmobile's engine growing distant mixed with the increase wind gusts. Raul getting away?

Would the sheriff make Samson search outside now?

Boots clomped in the mudroom. It was over. The men had come back inside. She bent over and pressed her face into Samson's fur.

A hand squeezed her shoulder and she looked up. Bryce. "We need to board up that window now."

"Did you see him?"

"No. Just tracks." But it's snowing like crazy so they'll be gone soon.

"And the sheriff doesn't want to use Samson to track him?"

He pursed his lips and crouched to look her in the eyes. "It's two degrees out there and a possible whiteout is in the mix. Neither you nor Samson is in any condition to track someone. If it was Raul, he's gone now. Just like earlier today, he shows up and, by the time we're on to him, he's already retreating. We aren't going to be able to follow him tonight. I want to know what he broke the window with."

Bryce looked around the room. Samson was sniffing at something on the bed.

Sierra gasped. "It's just a rock." She held her breath.

Did it have a note attached?

Bryce carefully lifted the rock to find a slip of paper affixed, held within a Ziplock bag to make sure moisture didn't destroy it.

"What does it say, Bryce?" Raul was going to a lot of trouble to keep her in fear.

He frowned. "Let's let your sheriff look at this."

"Look at what?" Sheriff Locke appeared in his doorway, Barbara standing behind him.

He marched forward into the room with a big board. Barbara held the hammer and nails.

"Oh, I'm so sorry, Sheriff," Sierra stepped forward. "This happened because I'm here."

"Nothing to apologize for." The sheriff grabbed the rock and peeled the taped Ziplock bag off.

He carefully opened the bag and slid the note out. The fewer fingerprints on it, the better, even though they knew who'd thrown the rock—and he'd likely worn gloves, given the current weather. The sheriff quietly read the note, then cleared his throat. "It says 'I'm coming for you.' Just more intimidation tactics," the sheriff said. "He wants to win a psychological battle and keep you buoyed by fear."

"Before he makes his final move," she said.

Sheriff Locke handed the rock and note off to Officer Kendall who had entered the room. The state officer placed it on the dresser and assisted the sheriff with boarding up the window. Barbara slipped into the bathroom to reassure Turner and Hooch.

John stumbled through the doorway looking like he'd slept like a rock through the whole thing. "What's going on?"

"Oh, Dad." Sierra hugged him. "Go back to bed. I'll explain tomorrow."

He gave her a look and Sierra quickly explained what had happened. John's features sobered and he approached Sheriff Locke to engage him.

Bryce tugged Sierra out of the busy room into the hallway.

He lifted a strand of her hair as if cherishing her, then cupped her cheek. "Are you okay?"

"As okay as I can be."

"The problem is that he's not going to stop coming for you. Right now it seems that he's willing to go through a lot of trouble just to taunt you."

Sierra agreed. "Why would he come here to the sheriff's home and not finish the job? How did he even know I was here?"

That much evil in one person sent chills crawling over her.

"All good questions." Bryce dropped his hand. "Let's get you out of here. I'm staying with you while they board up the window."

Sierra followed Bryce out to the living room where he put more logs on the fire. "You're right when you say he's going to keep coming for me. So I need to find him first like we discussed. We're still going to search for a cabin or a mine or someplace to find where he's hiding out, aren't we?"

Bryce leaned his arm on the mantel and stared into the fire, concern etched in his features. "Law enforcement is already searching, Sierra."

"But don't you see, Bryce, most of the people searching are not local. They didn't grow up exploring the woods and mountains around here. Help me to find him before he gets the advantage."

His gaze flicked to her. "And Samson? Are you willing to let him do what he was trained to do?"

Her heart wasn't willing, no. "Yes."

# ELEVEN

Tented vendor booths exhibiting ice tools, outdoor wear and gear lined the crowded walkway of the ice park. Spectators in coats and knit caps and beanies gathered to watch the ice climbing events featuring competitors climbing the frozen waterfalls of the gorge.

Bryce kept Sierra close at his side as they meandered through the exhibits, people on every side of them. If he weren't so focused on trying to protect her in this ridiculous scenario, he might enjoy actually watching the competitors scale the ice in the variety of contests including speed climbing.

But his priorities required he focus completely on protecting Sierra from Raul, and searching for the man in the process. State law enforcement was present as well, some dressed in uniform and others in plain clothes—everyone here to spot Raul Novack if he showed his face in town.

Like Sierra, Bryce couldn't help but hope they actually spotted Raul today here in plain sight so they could get their hands on him once and for all.

When the toy store didn't see any customers, Sierra and John had made the decision to close the shop for a few hours so that Jane and Sierra's father could watch the climbers. They would reopen for a couple of hours this afternoon. For now, all the excitement was here. Everyone wanted to see the action at the gorge or browse the vendor exhibits. No one was interested in shopping for toys at the moment.

Samson stayed behind with Barbara and seemed to be on the mend. Bryce was proud of Sierra for allowing the dog back into action—for the second time in one day. Sierra was slowly getting there. Bryce hoped Samson wouldn't have to protect her against Raul, but if it came to that, he would be glad for Samson's help.

He still found it interesting that Raul hadn't shot and killed the dog in the woods the previous day. Maybe he'd missed, but at close range, Bryce doubted that. Many criminals had quirks and maybe Raul was willing to kill people but unwilling to kill animals. Bryce wouldn't count on that though.

When it came to Raul, conjecture was just that—a presumption.

They made it to the gorge area just as the competition was starting, and maneuvered their way to a rail so they could watch as a woman used an ice pick and crawled her way up the frozen waterfalls. He kept thinking back to the way Raul had escaped them in the cold, snowy, icy mountains.

He glanced at Sierra who was smiling, and for once in the last few days, he thought she actually might have forgotten an evil man was coming after her. Her cheeks were rosy from the cold, and a few snowflakes clung to her lashes. Warmth stirred inside him.

*Friends. You're friends and nothing more.*

But the way he'd slipped his arm around her and the way they held on to each other for warmth and protection might seem to those around them that they were much more to each other than mere friends.

Bryce planted a kiss on the side of her head. Oops. He'd acted without thinking. Sierra smiled at him as if she welcomed the attention.

*God, what happened to us? Why can't we be together? Catch a break? Something?*

He had no business thinking about it. Or even asking God. He knew the answers to

his questions—this woman had hurt him before because she hadn't been willing to take
the risk, and he wouldn't let her do it again.
He'd heard her plain enough last night as she
shared with Barbara her reasons for not wanting to be with Bryce. It was as he'd suspected
all along.

He didn't blame her. She had a choice and
she'd made it. He had a choice too—to protect her until this was over. Then he'd be gone
before he fell head over heels for her again.

Her bright blue eyes flashed at him then
at the climber scaling the ice, and his breath
caught.

Bryce loosened his grip on her just a little.
She'd be okay. He didn't have to hold her so
close to protect her.

There. That was better. His heartbeat
slowed enough for him to breathe.

"Bryce. Earth to Bryce." Sierra pretended
to knock on his head. "You're a million miles
away."

"Sorry." He refocused on the task at hand.
Being this close to her scrambled his brain.

"Can you believe it's almost lunchtime? I'm
hungry. Let's head over to grab food before
everyone has the same idea."

"Sure thing." He held her hand—just so
they didn't lose each other in the crowd, of

course—as they pushed through the crowd, bumping into a few people, but no one as nefarious as Raul Novack. One of the more permanent eating establishments was situated near the ice festival and crowds already gathered there, while others remained focused on the competition.

This town really exploded during this festival.

Hot dogs, fries and Cokes in hand, Bryce and Sierra found a table inside the restaurant.

"I don't think he's going to show up today." She said the words around a mouthful of hot dog. "I can't decide if I'm glad about that or mad. I mean, if he does show up here, then maybe we can get him and I can get on with my life and you can get back to yours."

Her brows suddenly pinched and she stared at the ketchup while she stirred a French fry, creating a figure eight. What was that about?

He wouldn't for one second imagine that she didn't want him to leave. But her words had that effect on him, as if she'd said she wanted him to stay. As for him—he wasn't sure how he would feel when it came time to leave her once and for all.

Time to change the subject. "I've been thinking I might like to get a dog and train him."

That brought her face up, her beautiful blue eyes widened. "But you're a PI now."

"So? Are you saying that since PIs don't have their own canine groups, I can't train a dog? Well, there are plenty of SAR dog rescue volunteers. I could get involved in SAR and other activities." It would be something to do. Something to take his mind off...everything else. Off Sierra. Then again, it might only be a constant reminder. "I see how you are with Samson, and I've heard a few stories since being here of his rescues. That must bring you a measure of satisfaction and the sense of achievement. Like you're actually accomplishing something."

"Stories? Who'd you hear those from?"

"Well that guy at the café who seems interested in you. I grabbed coffee from there and he regaled me. He seemed very interested."

"Oh, I get it. He was fishing to see if..." Sierra seemed to catch herself.

"Right. If you and I had something going."

Sierra sipped on her soda until the straw made the gurgling noise. "There's nothing between me and Miguel. Would you excuse me? I need to use the facilities, but I'm not finished yet, so don't throw my fries away."

She got up from the table.

Why had she told him there wasn't anything going on between her and Miguel? As though she thought he would care?

He should follow her and stick close. He started to get up and then glanced down at her fries. She wasn't finished eating yet. Instead of leaving the food behind, Bryce watched her walk to the restroom, and kept his seat. He wanted to see her smile when she came back and saw him guarding her fries.

In the lady's room, Sierra washed her hands. *There's nothing there between me and Miguel.*

Her words to Bryce echoed through her mind. Now why had she told him that? It wasn't any of Bryce's business if she was seeing anyone. They'd parted ways long before she'd moved and she hadn't seen or heard from him in the year since she'd been back in Crescent Springs. So what if she'd changed her number?

Sure she'd thought about him.

A lot.

More than she should or had a right to. But she'd seen the question in Bryce's eyes when he mentioned that Miguel was fishing for answers—Bryce had been the one fishing. He'd wanted to know if Sierra was interested in Miguel.

She thrust her hands under the dryer as if

the obnoxiously loud noise could drown out her thoughts.

If only.

Sierra shoved through the door.

A sharp pain jabbed into her back—unmistakably a knife. "Scream and you die right here."

The man belonging to the voice yanked her around the corner down a short hallway where the restrooms resided. The voice sounded raspy—was it Raul's? She didn't remember him sounding this way, but it had been a long time since that horrible night.

It all happened so quickly Sierra couldn't react to prevent it. All these people—it was so crowded that nobody noticed.

And Bryce!

The weapon pressed deeper against her shirt, just beneath her coat, making her wince. She had to do something now or the man would succeed in abducting her in broad daylight at the ice festival. At the end of the short hallway, he commanded her to open the door with the red exit sign.

How could she use this door, this hallway, her defense tactics? How could she get away? If she screamed he would kill her—she had no doubt of that.

Then as if anticipating she would try something, he jabbed her so hard, she almost cried out in pain. She was certain he'd drawn blood. The door opened up to an alley and cold air swirled inside the restaurant.

*This can't be happening.*

All those people in the restaurant. All the crowds swarming the festival and the vendor exhibits, and an alley was empty? But she understood—two dumpsters blocked off one end, and a van blocked off the other.

Sierra should have seen it coming. But she hadn't and now she was in the middle of it. She was law enforcement. She knew how to protect herself. And yet she couldn't use her weapon because he'd disarmed her with a knife.

*A stupid knife!*

In her peripheral vision she could see that he was wearing a ski mask. It wouldn't draw suspicion—it was cold outside, after all. But it succeeded in hiding his face from all the law enforcement officers searching for him. No one paid much attention.

She couldn't suck in enough oxygen and hyperventilated. Fear choked her.

*God, help me!*

Even Samson couldn't have prevented this. Sierra should be able to go to use the facilities without fear of an attack. But her dog could have at least warned her.

The man guided her down the alley, but instead of the knife, he switched to her gun, having removed it from the shoulder holster as he held the knife to her throat. She could feel the muzzle pressing into her side under her coat. Locked and loaded. Ready to fire. At such close range it would blow a hole through her.

She'd wait for the moment—that split second in time that Raul's attention was somewhere else—and she'd go for the gun. What did that say about her that she lost her weapon to him?

She let the fury at herself and the situation course through her, hoping it would drive away her fear, so she would be ready to act when that moment came.

He urged her forward to approach the van parked at the end of the alley.

Whatever happened next, she absolutely couldn't let this man put her in that van.

"Look, I don't know what you think you're doing. I don't know why you think you can get away with this, but—"

"Shut up!" He jabbed her weapon harder into her side.

And that small pain was only a small taste of

what he would do to her when he got her alone. He would torture her before he killed her.

She fought the weakness spreading through her limbs.

*No, no, no, no...*

They were fast approaching the van, but Sierra was losing control of her body—her mind going into shock.

"Don't worry, girl. You're not going to die. Not yet. I'll let you watch me torture that beast you call a dog first."

Anger surged through her, empowering her. Sierra threw her head back and head-butted Raul. Temporarily stunned, she took that moment to free herself from his grip.

She had to get that gun away from him. Her gun.

"You're not going to touch Samson!" She plowed into him, reaching for the weapon.

He brought it down on her head. Darkness edged her vision.

Raul yanked her up by her hair. Still stunned from the blow to her head, Sierra was powerless.

"Stop right there. Let her go!" said Bryce.

# TWELVE

Raul had his filthy hands on Sierra!

Bryce pointed the weapon at the man, even as he pointed a gun at her head. The man yanked harder on her hair, but she didn't scream. Blood oozed from her head. What had he done to her?

Bryce saw red. He blinked to clear his vision, but he still saw red.

He should take the shot now and kill the man and be done with it.

"Lower your weapon or I'll shoot." Bryce allowed all the venom he held inside edge his tone.

"I don't think so," Raul said. "You put yours down or I'll kill her."

Bryce's body shook but his hands were steady, his aim was true.

"Mommy, Mommy…" A little girl ran around the van in search of her mom and ran right into Raul.

Oh, no! Bryce couldn't shoot. Raul was momentarily startled as well and lost his grip on Sierra, who slammed her elbow into his gut. He lost his aim and the advantage he'd had over Sierra and Bryce. Bryce had the drop on him and fingered the trigger, his aim true. Realizing he'd lost his chance, Raul shoved Sierra into the snow and took off into the crowd. He knew that Bryce wouldn't shoot him in the back, or shoot into the crowd.

Bryce was relieved he didn't have to shoot the man in front of the little girl, but he was ready to give chase.

A woman appeared and grabbed her daughter. Screamed when she saw Bryce's weapon and blood in the snow. Sierra's blood. How badly was she hurt? Bryce couldn't lose Raul. But Sierra…

He dropped to his knees next to her, his heart in his throat. "Sierra, Sierra. Are you okay?"

She grabbed her head and peered up at him. "He hit me with the gun. I'm okay. You go after him. I'll be all right. You can detain him for me. We have to get him!"

"I'm not leaving you." Bryce got his cell out and called the sheriff's direct number to inform him that Raul was indeed in town. "We have to close the roads, whatever it takes to get him," he said. "He almost got Sierra." *Almost took her from me.*

Bryce ended the call but he could hear in his head what the sheriff might have said to him. *"I thought you were supposed to watch over her."*

The guilt could crush him, and he would let it—later. After this was over. Now it was time to make amends.

He grabbed her arm and assisted her to her feet. She leaned into him. "What kind of cop am I, Bryce, to let him get the best of me like that?"

"You're a great cop." What kind of man, what kind of protector was Bryce to let Raul get to her?

He escorted her out of the cold and into Miguel's café. "Wait, what are you doing?" she asked. "My home is across the street."

"I'm getting you out of the cold while I call an ambulance."

"What? Bryce, stop it. You don't—"

But he was already calling. The ambulance might have a tough time getting through the crowd, but it would be easier than him trying to get her to a vehicle to drive her to the hospital.

"Can I do anything?" Miguel rushed forward. He peered at Sierra, his concern for her sincere.

"Yes. A bag of ice would help."

Miguel nodded and quickly disappeared. He returned just as quickly with a big bag of frozen English peas and handed it directly to Sierra. "Here, put this on that knot."

She eyed him. "Thanks, Miguel." Then she pressed it against her head.

Concern for her filled Bryce. Fury at Raul twisted through his gut.

Disappointment in himself could paralyze him. She might need someone else to protect her, but he knew she would never allow anyone else—he was fortunate she allowed him.

A siren sounded in the distance. Miguel explained the small ambulance service often had to deliver people to bigger hospitals, but the nearby clinic could look her over and then if necessary send her to Montrose or Telluride. Bryce feared that would be the case though.

EMTs rushed into the café with a gurney.

"Oh, please," she said. "I can walk."

The paramedic looked at her head. "Do me a favor and sit on the gurney."

Sierra sat and then she lay down.

The woman looked at Bryce. "She's going to be okay, don't worry."

Words of assurance spoken without any real knowledge. "I'm coming with you," Bryce said.

"Who's going to drive me home later if you don't have a car, Bryce?" Sierra was thinking ahead, even injured. She had to be feeling that injury now, not only physically but psychologically.

"The sheriff or your dad." Oh, that's right. Bryce would need to let her dad know what happened too. The gurney was moving and Bryce strolled along with it and held her hand. "Stop worrying, Sierra."

She closed her eyes, but the worry lines remained in her face.

They lifted the gurney up and Bryce made to climb in.

The paramedic looked at him. "Can't you just follow?"

"No. I'm protecting her. I'm not leaving her. A maniac is out there and tried to take her."

And Bryce had let that happen.

Sierra sat on the edge of the bed in the clinic.

Bryce stood against the far wall, but in the small space "far" didn't mean much. She could feel the concern and protectiveness radiating off him. She'd tried to ignore it while the doctor had bandaged the small wound in her side where Raul had drawn blood while forcing her out of the restaurant. She also had a mild concussion from where he'd smacked her on the head.

She would gladly take that concussion over all the other scenarios that ran through her mind of what he'd have done to her if he'd succeeded in taking her away.

Bryce was here with her for which she was glad. But she knew that look on his face. He was contemplating, and it was something big that she wasn't going to like.

That, and…well, she was pretty sure he was berating himself on the inside. Neither of them spoke much because there were far bigger self-recriminations going on inside—and who wanted to speak those truths out loud?

When she could no longer stand the silence between them she drew in a breath, then said, "I'm not going to sit here and let you beat yourself up, Bryce. Just stop it. I agree that what happened today should never have happened, but—"

"Oh, you can read my mind now?"

"Of course I can. You're thinking the same thing I am. You're trying to figure out what you could have done differently the same as me. There's no time for this kind of examination."

Despite the pain in her head, she slid from the table and moved to Bryce, blocking him against the wall. In his gaze she saw that he felt trapped and for some strange reason, for the moment, she felt like enjoying the power she had over him. But she'd truly been hit in the head too hard if she was thinking that way. She took a step back but he snatched her arm and pulled her close again.

He held on to her waist as he inched forward and spoke, his voice shaky and barely audible. "I could have lost you."

He gently tugged her against him. Wrapped his strong arms around her. "I'm so glad you're safe. And I'm…so, so sorry. Please forgive me."

The tenderness and anguish in his voice nearly did her in, but she'd had enough of weakness for one day even if the reasons for that weakness couldn't be more different. Still, she allowed herself to stay in his arms.

Sierra inched away enough to see his face. He was much too close, but she didn't want to pull away. "There's nothing to forgive. Nothing. You hear me? I wouldn't want anyone else here with me in this, protecting me and helping me. No one but you, Bryce."

At the same time, she wanted him gone. He was in danger because of her.

Fierce emotion flashed in his eyes.

Oh, why had she said that?

*Because it's true...*

Sierra found the strength to take a step back. Then another.

That emotion she couldn't read in Bryce's gaze remained. "Let me take you away from here," he pleaded. "We can go halfway across the world if that's what it takes. Whatever it takes to keep you safe, Sierra, that's what I want to do. I can't..."

What would he have said? Lose her? Fail? She wasn't sure she wanted to hear. Her throat constricted.

"Look, I'm begging you."

Sierra frowned and shook her head. "I just can't leave like that, Bryce. What about Samson? What about Dad? I can tell you he won't leave his home or his store."

"Because he's stubborn like his daughter."

"Whatever the reason, leaving is something that's not happening. If you want to do anything to keep me safe then help me get Raul. Help me take him down."

A throat cleared.

Sierra turned to see Sheriff Locke. "If you two are done, I've come to drive you home.

I didn't feel I could trust anyone else with the job."

What he meant was he wasn't sure anyone would be safe in Sierra's proximity because of Raul's determination to get to her. "Where is home, Sheriff?"

"You're welcome to stay at my place until this is over."

"Have they finished gathering evidence from my home?"

He nodded. "They have. Your dad already gathered his things to go home. I made him wait for you though. You decide what's best."

What was best was fewer people in her proximity so there would be fewer people in danger. Yet, she couldn't leave Crescent Springs either. Her father wouldn't leave, and leaving him here alone wasn't an option either.

"Okay, then. It's back to town."

Bryce's disapproval was clear in his gaze.

# THIRTEEN

In the middle of the night, the town was finally quiet after today's festivities. Even the lights were out in hotel rooms.

Bryce finished hiking around the cluster of buildings that included the toy store and Sierra's apartment in the back, wishing not for the first time that Sierra would have stayed at the sheriff's home. Though Raul had found her there and quickly. He must be watching her somehow. Raul hadn't taken her out from a distance because he didn't have the sharpshooter skills. Or maybe he was just fixated on the idea that he wanted to torture her before he killed her.

Bryce had equally dark thoughts about what he wanted to do when he got his hands on the escaped murdering convict and menace to society.

As he considered their current situation,

Bryce hiked through the deepening snow back around to the street with his hotel.

Since Sierra refused to go anywhere, Bryce wished that she lived somewhere else besides this property on the literal edge of the small town. Their apartment next to a big empty wooded lot connected to the National Forest. In the dark, the location presented too many opportunities for someone to get to Sierra. And it was dangerous—as he knew since he'd tried to chase down Raul and had fallen through the ice on the frozen riverbank.

She would be safe when Raul was once again incarcerated—as long as he stayed that way this time.

Sierra was right, though—she and Samson might be the best ones to search for the escaped convict. He knew how hard that decision had been, and how torn she was—not wanting to subject Samson to danger—but in the end, he was the best dog for this job. His safety was ultimately tied to Sierra's, and she'd finally reasoned it out. They had to do this.

Tomorrow they would take Samson and go Raul-hunting. After the near-abduction today, Sheriff Locke had convinced the state to send Rick Kendall along with them, though he wasn't available to guard Sierra and John's home tonight. They were shorthanded and no one was available—except for Bryce. Tomorrow, he and Sierra would be just one of many teams of searchers looking for the escaped convict, but until now, the searchers hadn't been local to the area.

None of them knew the area like Sierra and Samson.

At the hotel, Bryce crept up the stairs and tried to keep quiet so he wouldn't wake anyone. For now he would make the rounds every couple of hours. He wouldn't get much sleep tonight, just grabbing cat naps as he could through this ordeal. If this continued through tomorrow night, maybe he could take Samson with him. That dog would smell trouble and warn him. But like Sierra said, Samson needed his rest if he was going to search and track during the day.

Inside his room, Bryce peeked out the curtains at the store below. Glanced up and down the empty street.

It was much too cold on a winter's night to imagine someone out stalking—except Raul had shown them he was obsessed with Sierra and that the weather and elements wouldn't stand in his way.

Bryce's concern was only tempered for tonight anyway because John had installed a top-of-the-line security system for the store and apartment—he'd had a friend come in and set it up this evening when Sierra insisted on going home. Bryce wondered why it had taken them so long to begin with?

Still, short of sleeping on her sofa or next to her bedroom door, there wasn't much more Bryce could do. Sheriff Locke had his other deputies changing out watching the town, the state had left a few officers here as others pursued Raul this afternoon, coming up empty-handed so far, but they still searched. And Sierra had a gun—though they hadn't recovered the weapon Raul had taken—an alarm system, a dog she seemed willing to allow to protect her, and she had Bryce across the street. Not nearly close enough for him, but there all the same. Physically.

But emotionally?

He sensed that she still cared about him in a romantic way and was fighting it, the same as he fought it. So tonight, there would be no late night chats by the fireplace that might end in a kiss. A kiss presented dangers of its own and could send them down a road where neither of them wanted to be. He shook off thoughts of kissing Sierra—he definitely didn't need to spend the night thinking about that.

Her life was in danger, and he wouldn't, he couldn't, let Raul get his hands on her again.

*God, please help me keep her safe. Please let us find Raul before it's too late.*

Bryce lay on the bed fully dressed, his alarm set for two hours when he would check the perimeter again. Maybe his footprints left in the snow would serve as a deterrent.

He bolted awake when his alarm went off, surprised he'd actually fallen asleep. He rubbed his face then peeked through the window. Immediately he spotted footprints not his own. Or at least he didn't think so. He hadn't tracked so close to the building, almost as if hiding in the shadows. It could simply be someone walking home or to their car, but his gut told him it wasn't.

Heart pounding, he sent up a silent prayer as he texted Sierra. He hated waking her but this could be life or death. He warned her about the footprints in the snow and to be on the lookout. To be cautious.

Then he pulled on his coat and grabbed his weapon. Outside, he glanced up and down the street. Peered into the shadows and obvious hiding places.

The snow had stopped and the moon shined bright tonight, giving off enough light for him to see. He set out to follow those footprints.

If this was Raul, he must not care if anyone spotted his steps. Or this could be a trap for Bryce. He would remain mindful of that.

He wished he knew where the footsteps had started but at this point, he could only follow and hope he would find whoever had left them. If it was Raul he hoped he found him and took him down once and for all.

He gripped his weapon and held it at low ready. He followed the steps around the end of the building and then behind it near the woods.

*Not good. Not good at all.*

Apprehension grew in his gut.

The footsteps did not lead to Sierra's apartment door. They veered sharply away just before the door which raised his suspicions. Bryce stood in the shadows and let his gaze search the woods.

He hadn't felt the telltale buzz of his phone to let him know Sierra had replied to his text.

But Samson's deep bark resounded from inside the apartment. Maybe he'd barked earlier and scared the lurker off. Bryce wouldn't be foolish enough to follow him into those woods again, especially since he was alone. But how he wanted to get his hands on the man. He almost couldn't wait until tomorrow and he hoped Sierra would let Samson loose.

The dog should be recovered enough to track Raul and if Raul really was here tonight, his tracks should be fresh.

Surely the man knew that, but he'd succeeded in escaping the other K-9s brought in by the police.

His cell buzzed and he read the text.

Samson barked and growled. He won't let anyone get to me. Don't worry.

Bryce chuckled to himself. Yeah, maybe even including Bryce. Though it wasn't his intention to get too close to her, emotionally speaking. Unfortunately he had to keep reminding himself of that.

He responded to her text with a reply of his own about the tracks and a promise that he would stand guard out here for the rest of the night.

At least until he thought frostbite might take his nose.

The door swung open and Sierra peered out. "Get in here."

Sierra and Bryce snowshoed through the woods with Officer Kendall, following Samson as he trailed Raul with a combination of tracking and air scenting.

Sierra was so grateful to have Samson. And now, Samson's sharp olfactory senses searched for Raul—or the person who'd walked uncomfortably close to her door last night. Their tracks were now gone with an early morning foot of snow, but something of the scent remained and Samson would find him this time. She felt sure of it.

Their small three-person search team had dressed in protective clothing like the crowd of winter sports enthusiasts in Crescent Springs. The public was aware of the escaped convict and warned to be on alert, but it seemed to Sierra that news hadn't diminished the crowd or their passion for this event. Fortunately the competition was nearing its end and today would be the last day. This evening or early tomorrow morning tourists, spectators, competitors and vendors would pack up and leave town.

Then it would once again be peaceful and quiet.

The sun had come out and she felt entirely too warm inside her jacket, but taking it off was not an option—it was entirely too cold out without a jacket, and she'd have to lug it around anyway. Despite the business they were on, she couldn't help but think about the beauty of nature around her. God's creation was nothing less than spectacular.

And Bryce in this with her—God had seen to that, as well.

She wasn't exactly sure what to make of it since she'd worked so hard to distance herself from him.

A cold wind gusted over her face feeling much like the slap she needed. Sierra reined in her thoughts and focused on staying in tune with Samson. Training him had taken up so much of her life and they had to continue to train to keep on top of things. Now that she was sending him out to find a killer, she wished they hadn't fallen behind on training the last few days. If she had it all to do over again, she would have been especially focused on the attack aspects. She still feared Samson would face a gun and Raul would hurt him again—fatally this time.

She'd let that kind of training lapse since living in Crescent Springs and instead had cross-trained for search and rescue missions, and avalanche searches. Searching for criminals just wasn't a huge part of what they would normally see near Crescent Springs and the San Juan Mountains.

The evergreens' trunks clacked together as the wind blew again. An entire hour in they had traveled barely a mile and a half over the harsh terrain and deep snow, which, all things considered, was actually keeping up a decent pace. They had to move briskly in order to keep up with her working-class dog, Samson. But then his pace slowed. At the base of Carmel Mountain, Samson seemed to have lost the trail.

Would he find the scent again? She eyed the woods, the rocky terrain filled with fallen trunks and snow-covered thicket.

Finally, Samson started forward again. Relief whooshed through her. Bryce pressed a hand on her arm. "Careful. We need to remain cautious. If we're closing in on Raul, he's even more dangerous."

True words. She patted her handgun in her holster just inside her coat and left her coat unzipped at the top so she could easily reach the weapon.

Samson started making his way down the edge of a ridge that left just enough room for him to descend. Sierra studied the drop. It would be a perfect "hidden" trail for someone looking to hide, but it wouldn't shake a tracking dog.

"Hold it," Kendall said. "Are we going to follow him?"

"Sure we are," she said.

"Do we need special equipment to safely get down there?"

"First, keep your voice down," Bryce said. "If Raul is hiding out somewhere near, we don't want him to hear our approach. As for climbing down, we can see what Samson does first."

Giving the dog a chance. Sierra appreciated that Bryce believed in Samson.

Samson still made his way carefully down, and Sierra took off her snowshoes, preparing to follow. She wouldn't leave him alone in this.

"What are you doing?" Bryce asked. "I thought we were giving Samson a chance to let us know if someone is down there."

"I need to be down there with him. Just in case." As she made the first step she eyed the bottom. Her throat tightened. "There's a mine down there," she whispered.

Bryce nodded. "Let's go then." Bryce looked at Kendall. "You coming? If you don't want to, then you could stay here and guard our exit. We'll signal you if we find anything."

Kendall wore dark sunglasses and Sierra couldn't read what he was thinking, but he gave a subtle nod—that and the fact he didn't budge from his position was answer enough.

"While we're climbing down, you watch the area. Watch if someone comes out of that mine," Bryce instructed the guy.

"I know how to do my job."

"Wasn't implying that you didn't. But we can't defend ourselves so easily if we're coming up on Raul."

Sierra missed any further conversation. She needed to stick close to Samson. Beyond the protection of a vest, K-9s had only their teeth and an intimidating warning growl. They depended on their trainers to keep them safe.

She stepped carefully. A quick glance up and she spotted Bryce treading carefully behind her. Samson made the bottom and shot toward the mine.

If she'd kept him on a leash she wouldn't have to shout. She tried to keep her voice down as she gave him the command. *"Hier!"*

Samson had heard her because he immediately turned and ran toward her. "Good boy," she whispered, knowing he'd heard her words of praise too.

Finally, Sierra hopped on the ground at the bottom of the gorge that was only about fifty to a hundred yards wide in places. Bryce wasn't far behind and he rushed forward then tugged her behind him. He pulled his weapon out and readied it.

Her heart jackhammered.

Could this be where Raul had been hiding out? In an old silver mine down in a gorge near Carmel Mountain?

They could all be in danger if they cornered him like this. At the same time, she would never be safe until he was caught.

Wariness curdling inside, Sierra swallowed the lump in her throat. She removed her gloves and ran her hands over Samson's soft ears. She looked into his big brown eyes filled with love and loyalty.

He looked eager with anticipation. He wanted the hunt. She could be sending him to his death.

"I never wanted to put you in harm's way," she whispered.

"Sierra…" Bryce said nothing more.

She considered what command she should give him, but Samson seemed to understand they were hunting Raul—the man who threatened his master's life. *"Zooch."* Find him.

Samson barked then dashed away. He ran another twenty-five yards then disappeared deeper into the mine. Bryce and Sierra followed him, their weapons out in front of them and ready to fire.

Her heart pounded.

*God, please keep him safe. Please, keep him safe. Please, keep him safe...*

He was on the front lines now. He barked, signaling her that he'd been successful in locating his target.

She wasted no time shouting her next command. *"Fuss-en!"* Attack.

Samson snarled. Bryce led the way into the depths of the mine, pushing past the broken boards that had been put up to seal it at one time.

"We're at a disadvantage," Bryce whispered. "Whoever's inside can see us, but we can't see him."

"Help!" A man yelped from deeper in the mine. "Help me. Call off your dog."

Samson had subdued him. But the dog was still in danger. He could still get shot. *Hold on, Samson.* Bryce rushed forward and Sierra followed, turning on her flashlight.

Deeper in the mine they spotted a tent.

Her heart jumped to her throat. This was it. They'd found Raul. The man whined in agony, his voice sounding unusually high.

She shined the light on Samson and the man he'd restrained, his maw securing the man's arm, subduing him with one bite, warning of more. Bryce aimed his weapon at the man as did Sierra.

The man groaned. "Please, call him off."

Lowering her weapon, she commanded Samson to release the bite. "You're not Raul Novack."

Sierra eyed Samson.

"He tracked someone all right," Bryce said, frustration in his tone. "All the way from the woods. So you were out walking around town in the middle of the night?"

The man held his arm and nodded. "Yes. Who *are* you people?"

"We're searching for someone. A killer." She stared him down, letting the fury wash over her in waves. Fury this man didn't deserve.

"I'm no killer. Your dog got the wrong trail."

Sierra approached him, tugging a bandage from her pack and she wrapped his arm. Samson whined and sniffed around in the mine.

"Did we?" she asked.

Bryce paced the small campsite and ran a hand down his face. "So we're off tracking the wrong guy meanwhile Raul is out there doing who knows what."

Realization dawned. "Wait a minute. That's it. Raul. He wanted—" She stuck her face close to the man's boots. "Are those your boots? Are these your coat and pants?"

He shook his head, fear evident in his gaze. "I don't want any trouble. I don't—"

"Then you should have thought about that before you agreed."

Bryce approached them. "Agreed to what? You don't think—"

"That Raul had this man wear his coat and boots so Samson would track him here." Sierra glared at the man. "What's your name?"

"Eric. Eric Green."

"Tell me what happened." Sierra planted her feet next to him but crouched where he remained cradling his arm after Samson's attack.

She wanted answers and now.

He leaned away from her as if she intimidated him. Good.

"A man offered me money to do exactly as you said and to stay here. This isn't my tent or my stuff. I had to stay here until you came. At first I refused. It was crazy talk. But he said he knew where my mom lived and…and… There was something in his eyes…"

"Why didn't you just come to the police with that information?"

"Because he scared me. I didn't want him to hurt my mom. You guys are here now so that means I can go and my mom is safe."

Officer Kendall appeared at the entrance. Apparently he'd finally decided it was time to climb down, just in time to hear the man's confession. "You'll need to come in for questioning," he said as he continued into the mine. "Also get that bite looked at. The man you helped is an escaped convict."

"I didn't know. I didn't know. I was scared." He threw his palms up in surrender. "Look, I didn't even take the money. I did it to keep my mom safe. And well, I thought he might kill me too."

"He's telling the truth," Sierra said. "But how did Raul get away? There should be another trail leading out of the cave."

"How should I know? He approached me days ago."

*Days ago...*

Sierra struggled to wrap her mind around that news.

"Raul did this to throw us off. To drag us away... Oh, no. What if... Dad!"

# FOURTEEN

"We need to check on him!" Sierra tugged her phone out. "No signal!"

She moved closer to the exit until she got one. Bryce did the same. Officer Kendall would take care of Mr. Green.

Bryce contacted Sheriff Locke.

Kendall contacted his superiors to let them know what happened and that they had items Raul had left behind, maybe for no other purpose than to throw them off. But why had he decided to put this plan into motion last night? What was so special about the date and time, if anything?

"Sheriff. Please make sure John is safe, will you?" Bryce relayed the information to the man including their concern about Sierra's father.

"I'm standing next to him," the sheriff said. "He's all right. I'll stay with him for now. You keep Sierra safe. I don't like this."

Bryce ended the call.

*Neither do I.*

"Let's get out of here," he said. "We don't know if Raul has planned something, or if he's watching us now."

"I've been instructed to wait here until I'm relieved." Kendal's tone let them know he wasn't pleased about this new assignment. "Evidence techs are coming to collect Novack's things and search for anything important we might have missed."

"Did you explain that this could be some kind of trap?" Sierra asked him.

"I relayed the situation, but I don't see how it could be a trap."

Bryce looked at Mr. Green. "What can you tell us? Was he planning anything? Why would he go to the trouble to throw us off his trail?"

Mr. Green shrugged. "He didn't confide in me. Nor would I want him to. Since you called to check on her father, anyone care to check on my mom? He didn't leave me with my cell."

"Officer Kendall, let him come over here where I get a signal," Sierra suggested. "He can use my phone to call his mother."

Kendall escorted Mr. Green toward Sierra in case he decided to make a crazy dash out of the mine and this was all a charade on his part. After he contacted his mother and confirmed she was grocery shopping and having an ordinary day, he handed the cell back to Sierra.

"I'm sorry about your arm," she said. "Samson's really a good dog."

While Sierra made small talk with Mr. Green, Bryce pulled Kendall aside.

"I don't feel comfortable leaving you here under the circumstances. Nor do I like the idea of staying here with Sierra, but I can't send her back alone. Got any suggestions?"

"I'll be fine. Deliver her to safety. I shouldn't have to wait too long for the evidence techs. I'll remain in communication and let you know if I see anything suspicious." Kendall had taken off his sunglasses in the mine and studied Bryce. "Look, I know the brothers escaped and they might be some kind of brilliant criminal minds, at least the one that's left, but I can't fathom what he could gain by doing this. Unless maybe he wanted to study your strategy and tactics. See you and Sierra working with the dog and go from there."

"And that would mean he was watching." Bryce had already come to believe that somehow, someway Raul knew what Sierra was planning next. He pursed his lips, making a mental note to check her cell phone for some sort of tracking app and her apartment and store for hidden cameras.

"I'll tell you what," Kendall continued. "I'll look around here some more first. Explore deeper in the mine. Shine the flashlight around before we make any decisions about who is staying and who is going."

Bryce nodded to Kendall. He couldn't risk that he would make the wrong decision in this so he found a signal and called Sheriff Locke again. The sheriff asked him for more details.

While he relayed them, Bryce watched Sierra and Mr. Green, who had now made friends with the K-9 who'd subdued him. "A fake camp or a real camp where he'd stayed and then used to throw us off his trail. He decided to do that days ago. The mine could be an easy place to be ambushed, or bombed, or too many other things I'd rather not think about. The point is that I don't feel good about staying here. But I don't feel good about leaving either. We thought we'd found him, Sheriff. Now…"

How…how had they ended up like this? They'd planned to track and find Raul, but instead they were here and Bryce could see no clear safe direction. Raul had made a fool of them. Bryce felt like a complete idiot.

*God, please help. What's the right thing to do? I can't fail to protect her again.*

"Dynamite!"

Sierra jerked her gaze to see Officer Kendall rushing toward her. "It's not old like some miner just forgot about it. It's new." He glared at Eric. "We have to get out of here."

She eyed the entrance. "I have a feeling that it's not going to be easy to leave. We should lay down some gunfire before we exit. Cover each other."

"This was his plan then. Trap us inside. He plans to blow the mine." Bryce turned narrowed eyes on Eric. "You said you didn't know anything."

"I don't." Eric's fear-filled expression confirmed his words. "I didn't know about the dynamite."

"You didn't explore the cave?" Kendall asked.

"I stayed in that tent hoping you would hurry and get here. I heard someone coming so I came out and that's when the dog attacked."

They rushed to the mine entrance but hung back in the shadows. Sierra's pulse pounded in her ears, and she choked back tears. She didn't want to die in here like this, taking Samson and Bryce and two more innocent people with her.

Bryce and Kendall shared a look with her.

"Whoever goes first is going to be a target," Bryce said.

"I suggest we send the dog." This from Kendall.

Sierra fisted her hands. "No! He isn't expendable."

"Is there a way for us to stay here and survive the dynamite?" Eric asked. "Or can we move it? Throw it out of the mine?"

"I didn't look closely, but my guess is that he's attached a detonator—maybe activated by cell signal or radio attached outside the cave. I don't know enough about explosives to help."

"What's he waiting for then?" Bryce asked.

Good question. "I'm not willing to wait around and find out if he's going to blow the mine," Sierra said. "I'll take my chances."

"No!" Bryce's iron grip stopped her from going any further. "You're a better shot than me. You've always been better. I need you to cover me. I'll try not to get shot as I make a run for it. I'll draw the fire. You can try to take him out. It's up to you if you send Samson after him too. But get out of the mine. Wasting time on more words could cost our lives."

Bryce released her, then rushed out of the cave, without giving them more of a heads-up. She didn't have time to aim, so she fired her weapon into the ground, hoping her gunfire might scare off anyone gunning to shoot them if they tried to escape the mine.

Bryce made it to a boulder and so far, no one had accosted him. No gunshots could be heard from outside.

Sierra made to step out, but Kendall held her this time. "No. He could be waiting for you. It's you he wants."

"In that case I'd better get out of this cave before he decides to blow it up—with you and Eric still in it. I'll draw the fire and then you take him out." She twisted from his grip and dashed out of the mine entrance toward the rock where Bryce waited. This time gunfire resounded. Samson barked.

"Oh, no, Samson!" She made it to the rock, her dog next to her. "Are you hurt? Did you get shot?"

Then he sniffed at her and groaned. The fire in her arm drew her attention and she spotted the blood. Dizziness prevented her from telling her dog to find and attack the man after her.

Bryce continued to shoot at the ridge above them. Gunfire resounded like she was in the middle of a shootout in an old Western movie. Only this was real. This was today. This was happening.

An explosion resounded as the ground rumbled beneath them.

"Look out!" Bryce shouted and covered her using his body as a human shield.

Antiseptic accosted her nostrils.

Sierra opened her eyes to a white sterile hospital room. Grogginess held her in place, but she lifted her head. That elicited pounding and her vision blurred. She looked down the length of her body and found her arm bandaged, but as far as she could tell there were no other injuries.

She was alone in the room. Sierra searched and finally found the call button and pressed it.

A few moments passed before a nurse appeared. "Oh, good. You're awake. How do you feel?"

"I'll let you know when you tell me what happened to the others." Bryce. Samson. Kendall. Eric.

The nurse's expression took on a pained look. "I'll need to call the doctor."

Sierra sat up in bed and slowly put her legs over the side.

"Oh you shouldn't do that. You're—"

"What? What am I? Looks like you patched up my arm." Sierra started pulling the IV out.

Another woman entered the room. "Ms. Young—"

"It's Deputy Young and I want to know what's going on. What happened to the people I was with? Why am I here?"

"Ma'am, if you'll just calm down, Sheriff Locke is on his way to explain everything. He wanted us to call him as soon as you came to."

This wasn't the clinic in Crescent Springs. "On his way? He has to be two hours…"

She was shaking her head. "He's here at the hospital."

The aide entered and started taking vitals. "And there's someone else here."

"I'll go get him," the nurse said.

Another man. Bryce or her father? Sierra's head spun. What had happened? She eased back onto the pillow at the aide's urging. The images blasted through her mind as the aide put a pulse oximeter on her finger. Checked her temperature and blood pressure, which she was sure was high at this moment.

Bryce stepped into the room, bruised and scratched from head to toe, but beautifully, wonderfully alive. His smile barely hid the concern in his gaze, but she'd always loved his smile and it reassured her now.

He was alive. Her heart still hammered as he approached and took her hand, leaning in close.

"Bryce, you're okay. Please tell me what happened. Please tell me if—"

"Everyone is okay. Everyone made it out alive, thanks to you. And by everyone, yes, I do mean Samson too. He saved us."

"Where is he?"

"Well they wouldn't allow me to bring him up here since he's not one of the therapy dogs, though he totally could be. He's staying with Barbara."

"And Dad?"

"He's out there in the waiting room."

"Why am I here?"

"Surgery on your arm." He gently touched her cheek. "You risked it all to save everyone else by drawing the gunfire so Kendall and Eric could escape. Raul got a few shots in and hit your arm. Don't you remember?"

"I remember not feeling anything and then the explosion. I don't remember anything after that."

"Samson's a hero. He's a multitalented dog, that's for sure. He helped pull us from the rubble. After the explosion some rocks and dirt fell on us."

"I remember you covered me. You protected me. I remember that now."

"Yeah, well, I couldn't budge or move. My foot was caught. Samson pawed and dug and nudged until I was free. But you were… You were unconscious."

"I can't believe I passed out."

"Sierra. You were shot." He opened his mouth as if to say more then held back. "Fortunately help was already on the way. I was—" his eye shimmered "—I was worried you weren't going to make it."

Was he going to cry? So much emotion poured from him that she had to look away. She closed her eyes as if tired. She *was* tired. Exhausted. Finally she turned her gaze on him—she simply couldn't look away for long.

"Let me guess. They didn't find Raul."

With a grim look, he shook his head.

"So much for our expedition. I doubt they'll let us search for him again."

*Lord, why is this happening?*

She'd been a good and upright citizen. She'd done the best job she could while she was a detective and now here as a deputy. Why did evil hunt her down? She couldn't help the tears that burned down her cheeks. Though her eyes were closed, she knew when Bryce sat on the bed. He gathered her in his arms.

"We have to stop meeting like this. You holding me because something's wrong." She said the words into his chest, but held on as if for dear life.

A throat cleared.

The sheriff again. "I keep interrupting you two, it seems."

Bryce released her. Sheriff Locke crossed his arms. "It's good to see you, Sierra."

Barbara stepped in behind him.

"Wait. I thought you were watching Samson?"

She smiled. "I am." She stepped aside and Samson barked as he bounded into the room. He rushed forward and practically jumped on the bed.

Sierra hugged his big fat head and he licked her face. What would the nurse say? "I thought he couldn't come in because he's not a therapy dog."

"I'm the sheriff's wife, and I say he's a therapy dog. I can see that you needed therapy. Bringing him was the right thing."

Warmth flooded her heart. All these people who cared. Dad poked his head in the room too. "Finally you're awake."

"Good to see you too, Dad. When can I get out of here?"

# FIFTEEN

Six days had passed since they'd seen any sign of Raul. Bryce feared letting himself relax. Was this the quiet before the storm? Or had Raul used up the last of his determination to torture and eventually kill Sierra? Having failed, was it possible he'd decided to move on?

Bryce hoped, but again, he would stay alert.

Sierra had been released from the hospital the day after her surgery. He tried hard not to think of that moment when the dynamite had blown and rocks came down on them. He kept the details of that experience to himself. Sierra didn't need to know that she could have bled out before help had arrived, even before he was in a position to tourniquet her arm. The bullet had gone through the humerus and lacerated a vein. If it had hit an artery, she probably would have died. But help had arrived and whisked her away. Doctors repaired the vein and had given her blood to replace what she'd lost.

That was just another of too many close calls for comfort.

And now… Nothing from the villain in their life.

In spite of his wariness, Bryce had enjoyed the predictable uneventful last few days. As for Sierra's position as a deputy, she'd been put on a paid leave. With her injury it was best she wait a few weeks until the doctor okayed her to officially return to work.

But even if she'd been completely fit, Sierra wasn't going to return as a deputy until Raul was caught or proven to be far from this region of the world—that per Sheriff Locke, who said he would put her on desk duty if Raul was still at large by the time she was fully recovered. Sierra preferred working at the toy store if she couldn't get out there in the county.

So every day Bryce hung out at the toy store. Every day it was the same. Coffee and breakfast with Sierra and John, and then Jane arrived and they stocked toys and helped customers.

But today was different.

Sierra leaned against the wall outside at the back of the building and talked Bryce through training games with Samson. The sun shined down on the world and it seemed that no evil could break through. He knew better, of course, but they needed this moment of smiles and the feeling that all was well with the world.

Samson jumped around and played like a puppy, without seeming aware of how huge he was. He accidentally knocked Bryce on his rear. "Did you do that on purpose?"

Sierra's laugh was filled with joy. Only for this moment in time, and Bryce would treasure it. Samson held Bryce to the ground and he couldn't get up. He allowed himself a laugh too. "Okay, would you call your dog off? Come on, Samson. Come on, boy."

"Here." Sierra used the German command. Samson seemed to know this was more a game than actual training and he licked Bryce across the face and dropped drool for good measure.

Sierra offered her good hand as if to help him up. He grinned and considered pulling her down with him, but he didn't want to hurt her arm. He hopped up on his own and ended up standing close.

He stared down into her gorgeous blue eyes. It took all his willpower to keep from pulling her against him and kissing her thoroughly—after wiping off the drool, of course. He chuckled inside. He could live with weaving his fingers through her long golden hair, but Bryce held back.

If this was any other situation, Bryce would have already left.

John opened the door. "Sierra. I need your help."

"Sure, Dad. I'll be right there." She smiled and left Bryce outside with Samson.

"Come on, boy. Let's go inside too." Bryce needed to wipe the drool off anyway.

*What am I going to do?*

Bryce couldn't stay in Crescent Springs forever. He simply couldn't afford to keep renting a room in the hotel without dipping into his retirement. At some point too, he'd have to start building his business back up. He'd already turned down quite a few investigation jobs. Still he wasn't too worried. He had connections and believed he could drum up business again. He'd find a way to make it work, if that was what Sierra needed him to do.

Nothing was more important than protecting Sierra.

But it seemed as if Raul had disappeared. Law enforcement had scoured the area with no results, and eventually the number of searchers had decreased. Now it was a matter of citizens calling an eight-hundred number if they spotted Raul. The state had even used one drone. Just one. Sheriff Locke was trying to raise funds to buy one for the county, but politics interfered. Always politics.

So in the meantime, he was left with waiting and watching.

He and Sierra had both believed that Raul's incarceration was the only way she would ever be safe. But now what? Would they grow complacent and then he would strike?

Was that what he was waiting on?

Or maybe he'd moved on after his attempt to draw them into the mine and blow them to bits had failed. Maybe he'd decided his efforts were futile.

Still, a fugitive was out there. A dangerous fugitive who'd targeted Sierra.

Bryce sighed.

He'd move here if he could, but he doubted Sierra would allow him to stay and protect her indefinitely.

He pinched his nose and squeezed his eyes shut, wishing he knew what to do next. At the sink he grabbed a glass of water as if this were his place too. Sierra and John moved from the store back into the apartment in what bordered on a heated discussion.

"No, Dad. You don't need to do it. I'll do it. I can do it. I'm not an invalid."

"Well, at least have Bryce drive you then."

He downed the water, then said, "I heard my name. How can I be of service?"

"We need some supplies. Stuff we can only get in Montrose," Sierra explained. "It's about an hour's drive."

"She just doesn't want me to drive because she doesn't trust me."

"It's a treacherous road, Dad. I don't want to drive it either. Not in the winter. Are you up for driving the Million Dollar Highway, Bryce?"

Highway 550, aka the Million Dollar Highway. The only way to get to Montrose from Crescent Springs. It required one hundred percent concentration in the summer, but even more so during the winter.

"Of course. I might as well be of some use."

"Don't beat yourself up," she said. "It's better that we aren't getting shot at or stalked or attacked."

Sierra took a few steps closer and smiled up at him. "Don't try to deny it, you're bored out of your mind here at my little store in Crescent Springs."

"Me? Never."

And she was happier than he'd ever seen

her in Boulder. Carefree, despite the knowledge that Raul was still out there. But he looked closer behind all the warm fuzzies and saw that the wariness remained. She couldn't so easily shake the fear.

He tugged his keys from his pocket.

John tossed him his own keys. "Take the truck so you'll have room for everything on the list."

Bryce grabbed his coat.

Sierra dropped her hand to Samson's big forehead and rubbed his fur. "You'll be fine here, Samson. You're such a good boy. I promise, as soon as my arm is good to go, it'll be you and me playing again."

"Hey, I thought we had a good time." He gave a fake look of disappointment.

She glanced up at Bryce and sent him a teasing smile. "Too good a time. I was jealous." She winked—her beautiful eyes bright and hair shining...

He shook off the thoughts.

"You ready?" she asked.

"As I'll ever be." He peered out the window. The beautiful day they'd experienced had disappeared and a dark, gray snow cloud had moved in quickly.

Outside the store, they trudged down the sidewalk to find her father's truck. He opened the door, started the engine and cranked up the heat. Then he took one side and Sierra took the other and they scraped the snow from the windshield.

Once inside the truck he steered them through the small town and headed out on the Million Dollar Highway. Sierra seemed oddly quiet considering her earlier cheerful mood. Almost as if she had something on her mind and wasn't ready to talk about it.

He was glad, actually, because he needed to focus solely on the road now. There was no guardrail. Nothing but a huge drop.

"Why were those supplies so important again? Scratch that. Don't tell me."

"Okay I won't. But I do need to talk to you about something."

Couldn't this wait for another time? But he kept that thought to himself. He'd wanted her to speak her mind earlier and now she was ready. But why did it have to be now when he needed to concentrate on these switchbacks? He wouldn't be surprised if they closed the road at some point today. He hoped that wouldn't happen at a point when the two of them would have to wait it out.

"So what's on your mind?"

He steered slowly around the curve in the road to stare down at a big RV coming toward him. Was there enough room for both of them on this narrow two-lane road?

"Raul hasn't targeted me in a week now. I think he realizes it's taking too much of his time and energy and he's risking getting caught the longer he stays. The bottom line… You can't stay and protect me forever, Bryce. Even if I was paying you, I couldn't afford you forever. Just like you can't afford to work for nothing—not for much longer anyway. I think we both know that it's time for you to go home."

Bryce hugged the edge of the cliff as he slowly passed the RV in the opposite lane, the sheer stress of the situation combined with her words caused an ache in his chest. He couldn't breathe a sigh of relief once they'd successfully driven beyond that too-big vehicle—too big for this road, in his opinion.

"What? You don't have anything to say?" she asked.

"I'm thinking." He wasn't sure what he thought, except that he was surprised at the hurt that surfaced. She really wanted him to go?

A vehicle in the rearview mirror moving too fast for comfort drew his attention. "I'm not going to have time to respond. You need to hang on."

"Hang on. What? Why?"

"There's no way that SUV behind us is planning to pass. There's no passing here. I think…"

The white SUV didn't swerve into the left lane but continued pressing in behind them, faster and closer.

Bryce braced himself for impact even as he accelerated.

"Bryce!"

Heart pounding, she squeezed the armrests as though they could protect her.

The vehicle behind them bumped them slightly but Bryce continued to speed up so the impact was minimal. But he couldn't go much faster without their truck tumbling over the side. This road had no guardrail, but she doubted even a guardrail would protect them. They would go right through at this speed.

"What are we going to do?" Her voice was high-pitched with fear.

She risked a glance at Bryce. Tight lines carved his face as he concentrated on the road. She didn't know if he could get them out of this alive. If he could save them.

What could she do to help? Maybe keep quiet so he could focus. She looked around to see if she could spot anything they could use to their advantage. The road had been plowed but it had started snowing again after a beautiful blue-sky morning. Snow wasn't so bad but she felt the slight slipping every time the truck hit icy patches. Hitting one too fast could get them killed.

*Lord, please help us!*

"Brace yourself. He's gaining on us again."

"What? Well, can't you do something?" She regretted spewing out the words going through her mind.

"What would you like me to do? I take this too fast and we can't make the turns."

"I know, I know. Sorry. So what's your strategy then?"

"Stay alive."

"I'm glad to hear it." *Okay, Sierra. Just stop talking.*

"All I have to do is stay on the road beyond this next treacherous section and then our chances of escaping will increase."

She stared ahead at the huge straight-down drop into a rocky abyss.

"Here he comes again."

"That could cause us to nosedive over the ledge."

The vehicle slammed them from behind and Sierra's body jerked forward, the seat belt keeping her in place.

Bryce swerved around a corner fast, yanking the wheel to bring them back across the barely visible double yellow line into his own lane just in time to miss an oncoming vehicle. Loud honking ensued then fell away.

The vehicle was still coming. Still behind them. The driver was crazy and was risking his own life as well. Didn't he realize that? Did he believe he had it all under control or that he was invincible?

Or did he not care that he might die as long as he got to kill her in the process?

Sierra pressed her feet into the floorboard as though she was pressing the brakes and could slow the car—somehow it helped her psychologically. Her heart in her throat, Sierra was sure her life would pass before her eyes at any moment.

She'd thought she would die that night she'd looked into Raul's eyes as he'd pinned her to her bed and breathed his foul words of death, describing every evil thing he would do to her before he slowly killed her. She'd wanted to fight back but had been powerless. Instead she'd squeezed her eyes shut and turned her head away. Projected her mind anywhere but there at that moment, beneath the monster murderer.

Terror like she'd never known had paralyzed her.

What kind of cop was she anyway?

And now, she could almost feel that same terror bearing down on the both of them.

"I see it. I see what you're trying to make!" Up ahead, she could see mountain and trees on *both* sides so if they were run off the road, they could hit a tree instead of diving to their death. Still not a great option, but better than the road they'd have to pass through first, hugging the mountain on one side and dropping off hundreds of feet on the other.

"Unfortunately he sees it too. You might want to close your eyes, Sierra. Maybe even say your prayers."

"Oh, Bryce. Don't say that. Don't think like that." Though she was definitely already saying her prayers. But they were not prayers that one might say as their life ended. Instead, they were prayers of victory and desperation.

*Save us God!*

The impact thrust them forward and the truck slid across a sheet of ice.

Bryce shouted as he tried to gain control. "Come on!"

She risked a peek from her closed eyes. They were spinning—the ice had them and wasn't going to let go until it was much too late.

Nausea swirled in her stomach. Sierra screamed. Her heart stumbled around as though trying to find the right rhythm—the right response before they plunged to the bottom of the ridge. Time seemed to slow—she glanced at the movie playing before her.

The red mountain.

The snow.

The trees.

The beautiful and treacherous rocky drop.

Bryce had lost control and wouldn't get it back.

If she was going to die, she wouldn't close her eyes this time.

She spotted the vehicle that had sent them on the death spin sitting stopped in the middle of the road.

She caught a flash of *him*.

A glimpse of his face.

Felt the rage and fear he wanted to inflict on her.

The truck suddenly stopped, coming to rest against the rocky shelf that climbed above them instead of diving off the ledge and dropping a hundred feet or more. Her heart still pounding, she gasped for breath.

The nausea subsided.

"We're not going to die today, Bryce." Her words were breathy, but there was iron beneath them. "Get out," she said.

"Huh?" Bryce glanced her way, his face twisted in confusion.

"Get out of the truck."

# SIXTEEN

Bryce did as he was told. She was thinking clearly and was right. If they remained in the truck they would be trapped. Now was their chance to escape. He threw open the door and clamored out. Pulled her across the seat to get out on his side, since she couldn't open her door —it was pinned against the rocky ridge looming over them.

"Come on." Together they ran around to the other side of the truck.

She pulled out her weapon, and so did he. Bryce noticed her pained expression as she tried to use both arms.

Gunfire ensued, only not from their guns.

Raul stood in the middle of the street— snow falling around him and on him, cold embracing him. The wintry backdrop and long, deadly fall mere feet behind him.

Sirens rang out in the distance. Someone had called 911, or had Sierra? He honestly couldn't recall, he'd been so intent on keeping the truck on the road.

But this would be over long before anyone could come to their aid.

He edged around the truck. A bullet pinged against it.

Sierra's hands pulled him back. "Don't get yourself killed. Don't do it, Bryce. Not for me."

"I'm pretty sure he's going to shoot us both if we let him. Like you said before, we have to be proactive."

They'd thought the man had moved on, but he'd shown up here today like he knew exactly where they would be. It was time—past time—to end this.

Then Raul emptied rounds into the vehicle as Bryce pushed Sierra back, back, back to the far side behind the front right tire. The truck provided good cover, but it wasn't foolproof. Some bullets were bound to make it through.

"I'm worried about any innocent people standing by. Cars are already lining up along both sides." He realized several were honking. He'd completely blocked out the sound as he focused on surviving.

Didn't they see a crazy man had a gun and was shooting?

"I really don't want to engage him in a

gunfight in public like this," he said. "People could get hurt."

Bryce glanced to the ridge behind them. It opened up about ten yards away to trees and rocks—the portion of the road he'd been hoping to reach in the truck. Could they make it that far on foot before Raul was on them? And if they did, what would they do—just cower again? He wanted to stand out there and face off with this jerk, but his most important responsibility was to protect Sierra. Second to that, he wanted to keep any bystanders from harm.

Sierra had pulled out her cell and pressed it to her ear. "Sheriff," her voice shook. "We're pinned here on the highway. Raul is standing in the road shooting at us."

"Take him out!"

Bryce heard the words shouted over the cell. That was all he needed. What he'd been waiting for.

"You got it." He stepped away from the truck and aimed his weapon to shoot to kill, but Raul was nowhere to be seen.

"What?"

Raul wasn't in the vehicle. He… He'd just vanished.

A car at the end of the line of waiting commuters backed up, turned around and sped away. A man stood at the side of the road, his hands on his head.

Had Raul just hijacked his car?

A SWAT helicopter swept toward them and hovered in midair.

Bryce and Sierra put down their weapons lest there be any confusion about what had just happened. Bryce pushed her behind him.

"Call the sheriff again. Make sure he's communicating with these guys. Tell him that Raul took off in a red crossover—that he hijacked a car to escape."

"Okay." Sierra called again and explained. "Please tell them we're not the bad guys here. That he tried to kill us again and almost succeeded."

She ended the call and pressed her hand onto Bryce's shoulder.

Sirens grew louder, and a Colorado State Patrol vehicle expertly maneuvered around cars and parked next to the vehicle Raul had driven. It was probably also hijacked or at least stolen. What had he done with the driver?

Another vehicle pulled in behind the troopers. Sheriff Locke hopped out and rushed up to the state officers, telling them Bryce and Sierra had been attacked. His form was intimidating and he didn't back down even when facing off with state LEO. He approached, his expression filled with concern. "Are you okay?"

Bryce stepped aside for the sheriff to see Sierra for himself. She shivered and he turned to wrap her in his arms. "Give these guys your statement. We're out of my county now. Then I'll take you home."

"But… We needed supplies."

"All right. I'll take you into town and we'll get those, then I'll bring you back."

"Sheriff, that's too much trouble. You've done so much for me already. You have a big county to take care of—you shouldn't spend so much time on me."

He lifted his hat then sat it back on his head. "You're part of the people entrusted to me, Sierra. Not only that, you're one of my deputies. Now, come on. You guys are going to get hypothermia standing out here. You can sit in my vehicle and get warm."

A half hour later, they'd given their statements to the state officers. Bryce held his tongue on numerous occasions to keep from demanding some answers of his own. He wanted to ask why they hadn't already caught Raul Novack and put him back where he belonged.

Sheriff Locke would drive them all the way into Montrose to get supplies. While they waited on him to finish up a conversation with one of the patrol officers, Bryce sat in the back with Sierra. They watched as traffic once again flowed, only in a single lane around them. John's truck had been shot up and the engine was damaged, plus it would be used as evidence of this vicious attack.

Sierra's sniffles drew his attention. He should have been focused on her, but his adrenaline had long ago crashed and he was barely keeping it together himself. He brushed away tears from her cheeks. Her eyes widened as she swiped at him, refusing to give him the honor.

"I'm sorry. I wish I could stop crying."

Concern for her rippled through him. He wasn't sure he'd ever seen her so shaken, even the night that Raul had broken into her home.

"I thought we were going to die. The last time I felt like that, Raul was hovering over me, pinning me on my bed. So I just kept seeing his face and hearing his words."

She pressed her face into his shoulder and sobbed. Bryce held on to her with everything in him. "Shh," he whispered. He wanted to sob too, honestly. "It's good to get this out."

It was, wasn't it? Sierra was a strong person, but even strong people could be crushed, and it was best to let the pain out rather than to keep it inside. He knew that this was just the process that she had to go through.

Sheriff Locke finally climbed into the vehicle, and Sierra pulled away from Bryce. She looked up at him with swollen red eyes. "You need to leave."

They didn't have a chance to discuss her order right away. True to his word, Sheriff Locke had assisted them in getting supplies in Montrose and then ushered them back home where she could inform her father that his truck was toast. Once the county vehicle was unloaded, Bryce stood in the kitchen, looking like he was lost.

She understood. He was confused at her proclamation that he needed to leave. Sierra was spent. Her arm throbbed. She wanted to lie down, but she owed him an explanation.

"I have cowboy soup simmering in the slow-cooker if you want some." Dad eyed them both but said nothing more. He didn't have to. Anger was evident in his features. Anger at Raul. He probably had plenty he wanted to say to Sierra too, but he held back for now.

"In a bit, Dad."

Bryce.

He had to go.

"Can I talk to you?" She ushered him over to the sofa. Dad had a big fire going. He disappeared upstairs. Good. He probably sensed she needed to have a heart-to-heart talk with Bryce.

Samson made sure she knew he wanted in on the conversation, planting himself right at her feet. She hugged his big head to her and kissed him. When she glanced up, Bryce was watching her.

Bryce.

He was everything she could ever want in a man. But she wouldn't subject herself to more pain.

And that's why... "You have to go, Bryce. You could have been killed out there today. You were going to sacrifice yourself for me. You would have... You would have died!" Sierra realized she was shouting but she continued. "You walked out into the middle of the street to shoot him. If he had still been standing there, you would both be dead. This isn't some Wild West reenactment." She couldn't take the look he gave her and shoved from the sofa. Samson whined.

Sierra moved to stand near the fire and rubbed her hands. Her arm throbbed even a week after surgery.

Still Bryce said nothing in response. Maybe

he was waiting for her to get it all out before hc made some argument to stay.

"I don't want you getting hurt on account of me. Protecting me at the cost of your own life. I can't have that on my conscience."

Bryce was behind her. She could feel his presence. She wanted to escape. She needed to escape. But she couldn't make herself leave. She leaned back into him, resting her head on his shoulder.

"Please… Just leave."

He gently turned her to face him. "You know why I can't," he whispered.

And then he kissed her. All this time they had fought it, and now he pressed his lips gently against hers. The emotion that poured from him was enrapturing, and more than she remembered from before. It took her brcath away, and yet she knew hc was holding back so much more of what hc wanted to give.

She wanted to slide her hands over his chest and up around his neck and wrap her hands in his hair and pull him closer. How long had it been since they'd shared a kiss—years?

And why now were they finally giving in to that longing?

Back then, she'd pushed him away from her for emotional reasons. Now, it was so much more than mere emotion. "Bryce," she whispered breathlessly.

He eased from the kiss. "You want me to leave so you won't have to live with my death. But I can't have your death on my conscience, if I were to leave. I'm here until it's over. Whatever the cost."

And that's what scared her the most.

His breath tickled her cheeks. "And I know that I shouldn't have kissed you. I know why you won't let yourself love. You understand why I can't either. We're both broken in the same way."

She closed her eyes as he left her standing there next to the fireplace, listening to his footsteps.

He would leave now. Head to his hotel and perhaps get some rest.

As for Sierra, she wouldn't sleep after what happened today with Raul…and with Bryce.

She wouldn't sleep after that kiss. But he was right—they were both broken.

When this was over, he truly had to leave because she couldn't bear for him to stay. She might fall for him again and that was something she couldn't risk.

That night Sierra took forever to fall into a fitful sleep. She tossed and turned and would wake up and do it all over again.

A sudden shrill noise startled her awake. Gasping for breath she sat up and grabbed her gun, then realized her cell was ringing. She answered the call. "I'm here."

Silence met her on the line.

Then, "Sierra."

"Sheriff Locke, what is it?" The clock glowed 4:30 a.m.

"We got him." He was breathing hard. "We got him, Sierra."

# SEVENTEEN

Bryce didn't like this at all.

But he was in it until the end, and so he stood with Sierra at the jail where Raul waited for transport back to the penitentiary. Sheriff Locke had procured a way for Sierra to see Raul, hoping to give her some closure.

Bryce could not believe she'd requested to see Raul. A clerk hit the buzzer to open the door. Grabbing Sierra's arm, he prevented her from entering. "Sierra, are you sure about this?"

"Yes." Her grim expression seemed set in stone. "Yes. I need to look him in the eyes and let him know he didn't get to me. He didn't kill me or destroy me. All his attacks were for nothing."

Together, they walked down the quiet hallway—a gray polished floor, contrasting with bright green cells and bars. Every county jailer's dream decor. Their shoes squeaked in the quiet. Two state officers escorted them.

Sheriff Locke also accompanied Sierra. Raul had come after his deputy, after all, and terrified his wife at his home and his friends in his county seat, and the man was now in his jail.

When they reached Raul's cell, the man sat on the edge of a cot, hanging his head. Though he was jailed, his wrists and ankles were chained together ready for transport back to the penitentiary. Was that protocol for a dangerous, escaped convict finally retrieved, or were they making an exception for Raul Novack?

Raul lifted his head, his features somehow euphoric. When he spotted Sierra, a grin took over his face. He slowly got up and lumbered toward them. Bryce wished they weren't standing so close to the bars. He would remain with Sierra but he wished she would take a step back.

He understood why she couldn't. That would show weakness when she'd come here to show strength.

He stood close enough to her that he felt the slightest tremble in her body, and he put his hand closer to hers. Not holding it, just touching fingers. She responded.

Raul approached and held on to the bars, his chains clanking against them.

Sierra said nothing.

Had she planned to speak to him? Or just simply show him that he hadn't gotten to her?

Bryce wouldn't say anything, though he wanted to reach through the bars and do much more than say words to this man. He wanted to wrap his hands around Raul's throat. But that was the difference between him and this monster. Bryce would never act on such impulses.

Raul kept his grin in place. A grin that went all the way to his eyes. An evil grin.

"You're going to die."

Sierra's pinkie finger flinched.

"You're going to die, girl."

"We're all going to die," she said. "It's just a matter of when."

His laugh was sick. "And how, girl. You're going to die and I'm going to enjoy it."

"How's that possible now that you're once again in jail?"

He gave her a knowing look and just laughed. As if to dismiss her, he shuffled back to his cot, sat down and stared at the wall.

The officers ushered them back down the hallway. Sheriff Locke escorted them to his county vehicle.

Sierra didn't say a word. None of them did. Once inside the vehicle they all sat in silence. Sheriff Locke didn't start the ignition. He just sat there.

Bryce knew exactly what he was thinking, but Bryce wouldn't say those words out loud.

"What do you think he meant?" Sierra finally asked. "When he told me I was going to die and that he was going to enjoy it?"

Sheriff Locke started the vehicle. "I think he's crazy, Sierra. I thought you needed the closure or else I never would have agreed to arrange this meeting. But now it's over. It's done with. He's going back to prison and will be under extra security. The best thing we can do is forget about him. Forget everything that happened. Put it behind us. You especially, Sierra."

She rubbed her arms. She sat in the front seat next to the sheriff, and Bryce in the back, so he couldn't hold her. He stared out the window and watched the trees pass by and the day grow colder and grayer.

*It's over.*

*Just keep telling yourself that.*

Back in Crescent Springs, Sheriff Locke dropped them at the toy store. Bryce followed Sierra inside where she shared what had happened with her father and Jane—everything except Raul's words to her. John hugged her fiercely.

He gripped her arms. "Now you're free. He's back in jail. We don't have to think about him ever again."

If only it was that easy.

By going to face off with her stalker, Sierra had meant to make a statement, but in Bryce's opinion, things had gone horribly wrong.

She turned her attention to Bryce. "Let's take Samson for a good, long walk. It will be nice to do that without having to worry about someone attacking us."

He nodded. He hadn't taken his coat off yet, so was ready.

She led him out the back door of the apartment into blinding white. Fortunately someone had shoveled within the hour so they could easily walk.

Samson was leashed for the walk and they kept to the wooded lot, not encroaching into the National Forest. Bryce had so much he wanted to say to her about what had happened since the first day he'd been here, especially about today. He needed to process through his thoughts and he wanted that to happen with Sierra if only he could find a way to tell her. If only he could turn back time and prevent her from confronting Raul while he was behind bars. He wasn't so sure that Raul's threat had been idle, but how did he tell her that?

He didn't want to scare her. This had to end. And it should have ended once the man was put behind bars.

Since Raul had threatened Sierra, Bryce had a reason to stay. He *should* stay. He wanted to stay to make sure that Raul's threat wasn't real—that Sierra was truly safe now. *That* was the only reason. It had nothing at all to do with being with Sierra—her bright blue eyes and golden hair. Her smile and her laugh. The way she loved on her dog, Samson.

Or the way she'd kissed Bryce back last night. Bryce struggled to push aside the emotions battling inside him. He struggled to find the words to express what he wanted to say to her.

Samson took his time, seeming to enjoy the pleasant relaxed pace of the walk. He moved from tree to tree to see what was what.

The quiet between Sierra and Bryce wasn't their usual comfortable silence. Tension seemed to waft off Sierra. That could be Raul's doing.

Or it could be Bryce's doing. He needed to jumpstart a conversation. "When do you think you'll start training again?"

"Tomorrow, if possible."

"But…your arm."

"I'll make it work."

Not "we'll" make it work. It was now or never if he was going to convince her that he should stay on longer. "Listen, I think I—"

"It's time for you to go, Bryce."

Ugh. She hated the way those words sounded coming from her. Could she have worded this any worse? And the look on his face hurt her so much!

Stepping closer, she peered up into his handsome face. His silver-blue eyes and thick head of brown hair. "I want to thank you Bryce. No, wait. Those words are nowhere adequate. You saved me—so many times. I couldn't have made it through this without you. Of that much, I'm sure. But you don't have to stay with me now. You don't have to protect me. Raul is heading back to the penitentiary today."

Bryce's intensity overwhelmed her. She let Samson pull her away with the leash and averted her gaze to take in her surroundings of the beautiful San Juan Mountains.

Her home.

This was hard. So very hard.

"Sierra I'm not sure…" Bryce didn't finish.

"You're not worried about his threat, are you? Raul was just saying the words to freak me out." She paused to take in his expression. Serious. He was serious. And something more was behind his gaze.

It was that something more that she couldn't receive. Couldn't accept or explore. "I can't in good conscience ask you to stay. I would need to pay you if you stayed, and honestly I can't afford a bodyguard."

"You should know that your dad already tried to pay me."

"And you refused, of course."

"You didn't ask me to come. The way I look at it is that we're both in this together. We went through it together before and I would never leave you to go through it again alone."

"I can't thank you enough." She was repeating herself but she didn't know what else to say.

They stood close now. Much too close. Samson was sniffing the snow at their feet. They were probably the perfect picture for a romantic postcard.

Sierra saw in his eyes that he wanted to kiss her, but she also knew that he wouldn't.

"I'm glad you were here for me, Bryce. You're… It's meant so much to me. I hope you know that I'll be there if you ever need me."

He nodded as if finally accepting that she was right and it was time for him to go. Regret clung to his expression, but he too, knew that the moment had come for him to pack and go home.

Again she averted her gaze and this time squeezed her eyes shut. Images of yesterday accosted her. Bryce shoving himself from cover to take Raul out once and for all.

*For her...*

Buck's death came back to her along with the grief.

If... If she allowed herself to care deeply, if she hadn't lost the man she loved before to a bullet he didn't deserve, then Bryce would be the man for her. But telling him those words wouldn't do either of them any good. It would only lead to more heartbreak.

She'd already hurt him once.

They finished walking Samson, discussing mundane things like the future of the toy store. Bryce was also considering becoming a dog handler for SAR rescues. As they walked back to her apartment, they laughed like the two old friends they were, but Sierra sensed the sadness that lingered between them.

Right now, they were two old friends who needed to say goodbye.

Two old friends who might never see each other again.

In the apartment, he crouched and rubbed

Samson everywhere the dog enjoyed. "You're a good boy, Samson. Keep my girl safe, will you?"

*My girl...*

The endearment cracked her heart in a new place. Would that ever mend?

Sierra walked him out through the toy store. Bryce said his goodbyes to Jane and Dad. Sierra exited the store with him and stood on the sidewalk. Memories of their shared kiss surged through her, but she put those aside hoping she never thought of that kiss again.

Sierra stood on her toes and pecked him on the cheek. *Call me sometime*, seemed to be the natural thing to say, but she wasn't sure that would be a good idea.

His blue eyes were more silvery this morning as he peered at her. "Take care of yourself, Sierra. I'm just a phone call away if you ever need me. I'm in the hotel across the street until the morning." He winked.

Then he headed to his hotel to pack up and go back to Boulder.

Sierra stood outside in the cold letting the chill reach into her bones. Maybe it would chase the pain away.

Dad came out with her. "He's gone now?"

"Yeah." She shivered. "He'll leave in the morning so he won't be driving at night."

"Then what are you doing standing out here like you want to make him stay? Unless of course you do."

"No. I won't do that to him." Or herself. Parting ways the first time had been hard enough. A gust of wind blew cold over her along with snow from the rooftops.

Dad gently urged her back inside. "Are you going to be okay?"

"I think I'm going to turn in early." What would she do without Dad and Jane to pick up the slack on days like today? She could trust Jane to close up the shop with Dad. "I'll just go up to my room."

"Do that. I'll bring you some hot tea with your dinner in a bit."

"That would be nice, Dad."

Her heart throbbed along with her arm. Sierra might take one of the painkillers the doc had prescribed too.

Sierra woke and stared at the glowing numbers on the clock. Though it was still dark outside, it was already seven in the morning.

Bryce would probably wait at least until the sun came up to make that treacherous drive through the mountains back to Boulder.

Going to bed early and getting a long night of sleep hadn't removed the pain in her troubled heart. She and Bryce—they needed to talk about it. Talk it through. She'd thought she couldn't take the heartache of losing someone again and had pushed Bryce away. Well, she'd been right—she couldn't take the heartache of losing Bryce. The realization had been long in coming.

Maybe she didn't have to experience this pain. She wanted to avoid grief, the risk involved in loving someone like Bryce, but was letting Bryce walk away without even telling him how she felt any better?

Was that the answer? She thought the doubts would be gone by this morning, but they remained. Her pushing him away was definitely not the solution to regaining her peace of mind.

She had to catch him before he left. If she hurried, she could have breakfast with him and lay all her cards out there. Put them on the table.

Two old friends who potentially loved each other shouldn't leave things unfinished.

She groaned and rolled out of bed. Pulled her hair into a pony tail and finished dressing.

Downstairs, she was careful not to disturb Samson who snored loudly next to the fire. She didn't have time to walk him. She should probably text Bryce and invite him to breakfast.

But what if he said no or put her off? She'd hurt him, after all. Better to just show up.

She entered the toy store front, more doubts warring in her mind. What if she put her heart out there and he tromped on it, told her that loving her wouldn't be worth the risk? That… that would be worse than what she was feeling now.

*Come on, Sierra, have some courage.*

Sierra stood in the dimly lit store and looked at her phone contemplating a text to him.

The door jingled. Sierra froze. Had Dad or Jane forgotten to lock the door last night?

"I'm sorry, but we're not open yet." Sierra tucked her cell in her pocket. Never mind the text. She lifted her gaze to face the muzzle of a gun.

# EIGHTEEN

Bryce woke to his alarm, though it was still dark outside. By the time he dressed dawn would be lighting the skies over the mountain roads.

He rubbed his eyes.

Today he would go home.

But where exactly was home? Admittedly while he'd stayed here in Crescent Springs to protect Sierra, he'd kind of grown attached to the place. He'd actually started dreaming about a life with Sierra. Started believing she was finally ready to take a chance with him.

Because now he was no longer a cop but a private investigator and he could pick and choose his assignments and clients that wouldn't put him in the line of fire. She wouldn't have to be concerned about losing him like she'd lost Buck. Why hadn't he tried harder to make her see that?

Maybe subconsciously he'd become a private investigator in hopes of winning her back one day. So far he was doing a lousy job at that. His resolve that he wouldn't allow her to hurt him again crumbled away when he was with her. He wanted to take the risk with her.

She needed to know that, and she couldn't know unless he told her. He should have told her yesterday as they walked Samson and said their goodbyes. Those ridiculous goodbyes filled with unspoken emotionally charged words between them.

He threw off the covers.

Yes. Bryce was willing to risk the hurt all over again if it meant a chance with this woman who he'd never stopped loving.

*Admit it!*

He was so done with shoving his true feelings for her to the dark side of the moon. Somehow he had to convince her they needed to try again. Just… One more time.

He would stay here for her. It would be far from a hardship. This place was beautiful and peaceful.

He quickly dressed and rushed down the stairs of the small hotel. After his conversation with Sierra he could either check out or stay longer. Or find more permanent accommodations. Though wary, afraid to hope, he couldn't help the excitement that coursed through him. And as he pushed through the door of the hotel, dawn brightened the sky over the mountains as if reassuring him this truly was a new day and a new start for him and Sierra.

With a bounce in his step, he made his way over to the toy store. He'd planned to walk around to the back and knock since the store wasn't open yet. But he spotted lights on, so knocked on the door as he peered through the glass.

John emerged from the toys and let him in. "Morning, Bryce." The man had a quizzical look on his face. "What can I do for you?"

"I was hoping to speak with Sierra. Take her to breakfast."

John frowned. "To tell you the truth, I thought Sierra was with you."

"What? Why would you think that?"

"Well, she wasn't herself last night. And since she isn't here this morning, I thought she had gone over to find you and make things right between you."

While those words sounded good to Bryce, apprehension gripped him. "She's not here. She's not with me. Where could she be?"

"I don't know. Maybe she left me a note. Let's go back to the apartment."

"Or a text. Maybe she texted you where she'd gone."

In the apartment, Samson yawned and lapped at his water. Samson didn't appear concerned that his master and handler wasn't here. Surely he would have alerted John if there had been something to worry about. Bryce relaxed. She was probably talking to the sheriff about getting back to work. John had figured it wrong about how Sierra felt about Bryce.

John palmed his forehead. "Oh. I missed it. Right here on the table. She left a note."

He lifted an envelope and handed it to Bryce. "I was wrong. She left the note for *you*."

Why would she leave a note for Bryce? For all Sierra knew he was leaving this morning. But maybe she knew him well enough to know he would want to talk to her about staying one more time. Maybe that was why she wasn't here—so she wouldn't have to hurt him by sending him away again when he came for her.

His heart ached. He'd been rejected again without even trying. Note in hand, he quickly opened it and skimmed the contents.

Bryce,
If you're reading this note that means

that you're still here. Please know nothing can happen between us. Ever. I would like you to leave. If you don't leave town then it feels like you're more of a stalker than anything. I'm glad you were here to help me escape Raul, but that's over. I don't need you anymore.

"Oh." Bryce folded the missive and stuck it back in the envelope. He didn't want John to read it otherwise Bryce would have simply wadded it up and tossed it in the trash. Instead he stuffed it in his pocket.

"Well where is she?"

"It didn't say. Just…she was just saying goodbye. So I'll be on my way." He shook John's hand and told him to call if he needed anything.

Though John smiled, more of his frown stayed in place.

In a pain-filled daze he checked out of his hotel and loaded his vehicle. He sat in the seat and let it heat up, hurt squeezing his chest. Could she really view him like a stalker?

Why had he let himself care about her again?

He slammed the steering wheel.

*I knew better!*

* * *

She'd been stupid to not see this coming. She should have figured it out. Instead, she'd been caught completely off guard by her abductor—someone who hadn't been on her radar.

*Just a little more. It has to work. Just one more try.*

Gasping for breath, she growled in frustration and gave up. But she'd given up already too many times. She would try again.

*Breathe in. Breathe out.*

*In. Out. In, out, in, out, in, out.*

Okay now she was hyperventilating.

*Calm down. You can do this.*

She had to get out of here or she would die at the hands of her abductor. Sierra worked her wrists back and forth. They were tied together behind her around the chair back. It was painful to be tied in this position for so long, especially with her injured arm. The muscles in her shoulders and arms burned as if on fire. At least the circulation still flowed. She kept reminding herself that pain was good.

Okay. Again. She tried loosening the rope around her wrist. Rope seemed old-school when there was duct tape or plastic ties, but she would be grateful for small things. Wearing down plastic ties would be a lot harder.

Even with rope, her skin raw and likely bleeding by now, sharp pains stabbed with each twist to try to pull one or the other hand out. To try to loosen up the rope.

Had they taught her how to escape this in cop school? If they had, she must have missed that day.

What they *had* taught her, was how not to get abducted. Being fully aware of one's surroundings and ever on alert was key. But she just hadn't seen this one coming.

The wind howled through the cracks in the window of the creepy old cabin in the woods, making it seem haunted. Old logs that had been stacked together to form a square room sometime in the last century added to the unnerving feel. Sierra wasn't in the market for an old cabin—she was desperately trying to escape. But someone had clearly made themselves at home here.

Was this where Raul had been staying before he'd been caught?

She shivered as cold fear wrapped around her. That and a heaping dose of chilled air as the temps dropped outside.

How many hours would she have to remain tied to the chair in this ancient, decrepit cabin? The fire had died out long before she'd been abducted and brought here. Again, she'd worked her wrists back and forth. Warm fluid spread.

Now she knew she was bleeding.

She had already tried to break the chair. That, she'd done first—to no avail. She'd merely left herself bruised and in pain and almost knocked herself unconscious. Her gunshot-wounded arm throbbed incessantly.

How was she going to get out of this?

*I have to get out of here.* She gasped. *God, please I have to get out of here. Please help me. This can't be it. This can't be the end.*

Because... Because more than just wanting to live, she wanted another chance with Bryce. She saw that now. Early this morning, she'd realized she should at least talk about her feelings with him, but now she didn't even want to talk about them. She didn't want to reason or analyze or discuss. The time for talk was long over.

If she ever saw him again she would run up and kiss him good and hard and convince him that she was the one for him. She'd been so foolish to push him away. He'd walked back into her life and Sierra should have seen that for what it was—a sign.

Life was much too short to live in fear of loving because you were afraid you might lose someone.

She should have told Bryce how she felt about him when she had the chance.

And now it might be too late.

She'd been forced to hurt him all over again with that cruel, heartless note. Pain lanced through her heart.

*Oh, Bryce... Please don't believe it. Don't believe a word of it!*

Still, considering the history they shared, Sierra should accept the fact there was no chance he would read the note, if he even got it, and do anything but leave town.

*If* Bryce read the note, he wouldn't be coming to look for her.

And if he *didn't* read the note, he wouldn't be coming to look for her.

She'd made sure of that.

*I'm going to die...* But she wasn't ready to die.

She laughed hysterically at her desire to live. When did that ever make a difference?

# NINETEEN

"Look, something's wrong, John. Please let me take Samson. He can help me find her," Bryce pleaded. He'd driven nearly ten miles out of town, gearing up to face a tumultuous drive in the increasing winter weather when it hit him like a cold smack in the face.

"Sierra didn't write that note. She would never be cruel like that, dismissing me as if she didn't even consider me a friend. And the words seemed stilted." Bryce thrust the note out for John to read.

He skimmed the contents then frowned. Did John believe the note was sincere—that this was truly Sierra's opinion of him? That notion cut him through and through, but he pushed the pain aside. Time to care later. Right now he needed to convince Sierra's father. But how? He scraped a hand around the back of his neck. Maybe he should go to the sheriff, except that would take more time. He was here now with Samson. If the dog couldn't catch a scent and someone had taken her, then what would they do?

Panic swelled in his chest. He fisted his hands. "Every minute you make me beg you could have one less minute left to save her. You come too. You can help me find her."

The man frowned, desperation filling his eyes. "You don't have to convince me, son. I know you're right. Sierra wouldn't have written this note unless she was forced. You go and I'll call the sheriff. But I don't know if Samson will take your commands."

"I don't know either, but I've watched Sierra. And I know the dog will want to find her. He seems anxious right now as though he senses something's wrong." Though admittedly the dog had only grown anxious since Bryce had come in and started stirring up trouble. "Let me try. If she's anywhere near then Samson will find her."

"But if you're right," John said, "and she's in danger, she wouldn't want you to put her dog in harm's way. That was one of the reasons she moved back here."

"What do you think, John? Are you okay with me taking the dog into a dangerous situation if it means saving Sierra?"

"Go. Find her. Just don't let her dog get hurt."

Bryce leashed Samson, afraid he wouldn't be able to call him back. He needed the dog sticking close to him on their search.

He grabbed Sierra's scarf to let Samson know that Bryce wanted him to find Sierra. He wasn't a trained handler but simply copied what he'd seen Sierra do. He rubbed the scarf over Samson's nose. "Find Sierra."

What was the German word Sierra had used? His brain too flustered—he couldn't remember. Then Bryce opened the back door to the woods. They could start there.

Samson nearly yanked his arm off as he escaped through the door. Was it working? He cautioned himself not to get his hopes up. For all Bryce knew Samson had merely picked up on Sierra's previous excursion here. Bryce couldn't know and could be wasting time too. Then again, judging by Samson's urgency, he could very well lead Bryce to Sierra.

"I'm calling the sheriff." John shouted from behind.

Bryce followed the dog's urgent search through the deep snow, over fallen snow-covered logs, branches. Through the under-brush, and over frozen creeks. Samson veered south along the river where Bryce had fallen through the ice a few days back. Bryce feared the dog could lose the scent as he'd seen happen a few times—due to someone getting out on a snowmobile or because the snow-covered the tracks—but Samson continued on unhesitatingly.

Bryce sucked the cold air deep into his lungs—he might die of a heart attack before Samson found Sierra. But one thing he felt in his gut—the dog was on her scent.

"Good boy. Keep up the good work. Find Sierra."

*God, please just let this storm ease up, and let me find her. Protect her. Protect Samson. Help me to find and save her.*

He struggled to maneuver around boulders and over rocky outcroppings as Samson searched to catch a trace of Sierra's scent.

*Lord, help us find Sierra.*

*Better yet, just have her call me on my cell to say that she's all right.*

With the thought and prayer, he felt the buzz in his pocket. He didn't want to slow Samson down, so kept up with him as he dragged the cell out and tried to view it with numb, gloved hands.

"Hold up, Samson!" Probably not a command, but Samson whined, understanding just the same. He continued to sniff.

Bryce read the text from John.

Sheriff hasn't seen Sierra this morning. He'll help look around town and worst case, he'll organize a search party. She was supposed to talk to him today about coming back to work and didn't show up. Please find Sierra, son!

Finally, about an hour after they'd started, Samson alerted Bryce to a cabin. He tried to remember the command for Samson to sit and stay quiet. Bryce pulled his fingers from his gloves to ready his weapon, unsure if any part of his body would respond in this cold. If Samson could be trusted, Sierra was in that cabin.

And not by her own will.

What had happened? Who had taken her?

Keeping to the trees, he slowly approached the log cabin. Snow piled high on one side and he wondered about the reliability of the old structure. Dim light drifted from one dirty window. A branch hung low and scraped the window.

Bryce waited and listened, then slowly eased over to peek into the window, hoping the moving branch would help hide the movement. His heart lurched at what he saw. Sierra was tied to a chair, arms behind her back. Her ankles were tied too.

Her mouth had been stuffed so she couldn't

scream—as if anyone would hear her out here. Bruises covered the left side of her face.

And *Jane* stood over Sierra speaking. Bryce couldn't hear her words above the wind that was picking up. Seemed like they were going to get caught in a blizzard.

This was the moment of truth. Would Bryce be able to save her this time too, like he'd done in the past? Would he die for her? He was certainly willing.

To calm his pounding heart, he slowly breathed in a few icy breaths.

He sent up a silent prayer. *Lord, you never leave us nor forsake us. Be with me now as I go in to free Sierra. Keep her safe.*

Bryce wished he could simply command Samson to attack. But that could get the dog killed and Sierra would never forgive Bryce for putting her beloved pet in harm's way. Ideally, he'd wait for backup of the human variety, but there just wasn't enough time.

Jane's back was to him so Bryce took advantage of that and analyzed the room and surroundings. There wasn't any way he could enter the cabin through that one door without alerting Jane of his approach.

One step on that porch would probably give him away unless she thought the wind was causing the creaks. He could hope. The only good news was that the heavy wooden beam used to bolt the door was hanging down, and the door could be breached more easily. Still…

*God, what do I do?*

He considered his few options, indecision warring inside him. He didn't want Sierra to get hurt or killed when he entered. But he couldn't just stand there and watch her be harmed either.

Bryce had to act now.

Sierra stared at Jane, her eyes watering with pain. In her wildest dreams, she never imagined this would happen. Raul had been the tormenter in her dreams.

She hadn't known that he and Damien had raised a niece after her mother had died in a car crash. They'd changed her name and protected her from all connections to them. Her true name was Raven. But under the guise of Jane, she'd come to work for Sierra and planned out her revenge—long before her uncles had escaped and tried to do the same.

With Damien's death, Jane and Raul worked together to extract vengeance. And Jane had provided the hiding place for her uncle Raul at her own home right there in town.

Sierra wanted to heave to think that Raul's

niece, Jane, who hated her so much, had been so close to her this whole time. She had been close to thinking of Jane as family more than an employee. Over time she would have. What about the guy Jane was dating? Did he know her true identity—and her true, cruel nature? The whole thing caused acid to rise in her throat. Raul had been even closer than she ever could have imagined.

He had eluded the police and the search dogs with his snowmobile and other tricks, but in the end he always returned to Jane's home without anyone being the wiser. That is, until he'd been caught coming back from his highway attack. That had been one desperate and stupid move on his part, to boldly stand on that road shooting at them when there was no real escape for him.

All Sierra could think was that he hadn't cared if he was caught, as long as he killed her. But he'd failed.

"And now I'm left to finish the job," Jane said. Her entire demeanor had changed, and she looked like a dangerous and venomous person.

"It's been my show all along, really. Sure, Uncle Raul shot at you and attacked you, but I played the mind games. I ransacked the home while you and your good old dad were out."

That made sense, but Jane had seemed so

concerned for her when she had called to inform about the break-in. Why hadn't Sierra sensed something in Jane or seen this coming? Why hadn't she figured it out when Raul had seemed to know her every move before she made it? Because Jane had informed him of all of her plans. She'd been listening closely to all Sierra's conversations even though she'd seemed to be busy at work and happy with her job. And when she wasn't at work, she'd lived in a bungalow in a wooded area on the edge of town where Raul could come and go without prying eyes. But she'd clearly found a remote and forgotten cabin to use in her plans to abduct Sierra.

"You have no idea how long I've been planning and waiting for this. Did you know that I followed you all the way from Boulder?" She giggled as if punch drunk. "And when you hired me for that part-time job helping out at the store, I knew that providence must be on my side."

Sick. Providence would never be on the side of a crazy like Jane.

Jane pulled the rag out of Sierra's mouth. "Well? Got anything to say to all that?"

Sierra moved her tongue around and tried to wet her parched lips. "Why now? You've been here for a year. Why did you decide…

Oh, because your uncles escaped. But you didn't have to reveal yourself. Why continue? You'll only be caught just like Raul was."

That earned her another slap on the face. Jane must have been holding it all in this last year and waiting for the moment when she could unleash her pent-up anger. Again, nausea roiled inside.

"I knew that your boyfriend could end up staying. I wanted to keep taunting you, but I couldn't if he stayed. So I sent him away when I made you write that note. He must be miles away now and no one is coming to save you this time. My only regret is that my uncle—"

A disturbance drew their attention.

Bryce had knocked through the doorway. He pointed a gun straight at Jane.

"Step away from her and put your hands on your head."

Ignoring Bryce's demands, Jane laughed. "Well, well. You figured it out after all. I don't mind—I have to say that Plan B is just as exciting as Plan A. Now I get to kill those whom Sierra cares about the most right in front of her."

Jane darted away, dodging Bryce's bullet and producing a gun of her own. She aimed it at Sierra.

As if in slow motion, Sierra watched as a growling, barking Samson jumped on Jane but not before she fired her gun right as Bryce lunged in front of Sierra.

Samson and Bryce—she loved them both—tried to save Sierra. Jane was screaming. Samson subdued her with his massive form.

And now Sierra better understood what had happened. Samson had never liked Jane. Maybe he had even tried to alert Sierra, who continually trained him to trust Jane... So Jane had been able to march into the store and abduct Sierra at gunpoint without anyone being the wiser.

Including her precious guard dog, Samson. Tears leaked from her eyes.

"Call him off! Call your dog off!" Jane screamed.

Sierra ignored the woman. "Bryce, get up. Bryce, are you okay?"

He groaned. Got to his feet then produced a knife. Hands shaking, he cut her free. She rubbed her bleeding wrists. He cut her ankles free too.

"Are you all right?" she asked. "Wait, you're shot!"

He looked himself over. "No. She missed. Samson changed her aim."

"You risked your life for me again, Bryce. You could have died."

"It's all part of the—" he cleared his throat "—it used to be part of the job."

He kept his intense gaze on her, a gaze that could have been lifeless now since he'd once again risked his life, willing to give it for her.

This was why she couldn't love because… Because she couldn't take that pain of loss again.

But it was too late.

Sierra already loved Bryce.

Samson clamped down on Jane's arm to keep her in place. Sierra's hands were numb from being tied so long. "Do you have handcuffs you could secure her with? And let's call the sheriff."

He nodded. Stumbled over to Jane and secured her hands while Sierra tried to get a signal. Finally she found one bar and left a voicemail. Then she texted the information to the sheriff in case her words were garbled. Sent the text to multiple people including Dad.

Samson relinquished his hold on Jane after Bryce restrained her with the rope she'd used on Sierra.

"Samson," Sierra called. "Good boy. You found me, didn't you?"

"And you, Bryce. You… You came looking for me. Why? That note I wrote—I figured you would be long gone and I would die here."

"The note didn't sound like you. Either that or I didn't want to believe you in which case that would mean I *am* a stalker."

Samson moaned, then suddenly struggled to stand. He ignored Sierra's commands for his attention. What was happening? What was wrong?

Panic slid around Sierra's throat.

Her dog collapsed at her feet.

"Samson? Samson!" She held his head up. His eyes were closed, but he still breathed.

Sierra gazed around the room. Had Samson gotten into something? She spotted the water bowl over behind where she'd been sitting. She hadn't been able to see it before.

*No…*

Maniacal laughing started from the table. Sierra gazed over at Raven. "What did you do?"

"It's all part of Plan B."

To kill those whom Sierra cared the most about—right in front of her. Bryce hadn't been shot, but Samson…

# TWENTY

At the Crescent Springs Vet Hospital, where Samson lay on a table, they waited. A couple of chairs sat empty against the wall. Sierra couldn't sit while she worried about Samson. So she stood and leaned against the sterile decor, the fingers of one hand covering her mouth, the other hand held firmly in Bryce's. He was as concerned for Samson's well-being as Sierra was, and remained understanding and patient. She thought he might even be praying.

Sierra thought back to her experience at the cabin where Jane had taken her. To Bryce and Samson's heroic actions to save Sierra and capture Jane. Despite the blizzard brewing outside, the authorities had moved quickly for Sheriff Locke, deputies and Officer Kendall to get to the cabin to arrest Jane-Raven. They also brought with them an opioid antidote kit Sierra had requested. She couldn't know for certain that's what caused Samson's reaction, but Bryce had found a stash of pill bottles with painkillers on Jane. She finally admitted she'd crushed a few pills into the water as part of her Plan B in case Bryce and Samson decided to be heroes.

In this case, Sierra believed her.

How could Jane harm Samson like that? It took significant control not to unleash her rage on the woman. Unfortunately Jane was raised by two demented men and followed in their footsteps. But Jane was no longer Sierra's concern.

She focused her thoughts on Samson.

Proximity to Sierra had been dangerous to those closest to her, and now Samson could pay the highest price of all.

The vet, Harry Eubanks, had explained that dogs were trained to search for drugs and were more resistant to narcotics than humans, but those same dogs who could sniff out heroin could die from small doses of the synthetic opioids used for pain relief. Veterinarians, police and EMT's now regularly carried the kits to treat overdoses.

Harry listened to Samson's heart and lungs with his stethoscope. He peered up at Sierra. "It's been a couple of hours since the naloxone was administered to counter the drugs. All we can do now is wait."

"And pray," she said. She wouldn't leave his side until this was over, one way or another. *But God please let him wake up. Let the antidote work for him.*

She never meant for Samson to be put in danger. If Samson died because he'd come with Bryce to find and save her, she didn't know how she could deal with that.

As it was, she wanted so much to tell Bryce what she was truly thinking about the fact that he'd thrown himself in front of a bullet. But that conversation would have to wait. Now she was concerned for her best friend, Samson.

"He's going to be okay, Sierra," Bryce said. "Don't you worry. Samson's a strong one."

Sierra was keeping the faith, keeping the hope. She wanted to believe what Bryce said was true. She wouldn't argue with him about it. But when she glanced up and into his eyes, she saw the question in his eyes plain as day.

He feared that she blamed him for this. Bryce was the one to take Samson out to search for her, so in that respect he had put the dog in harm's way. But she didn't hold that against him—after all, if he hadn't used Samson, she would be dead right now. She'd been praying he would use Samson to find her.

"Tell me what you want me to do, Sierra. How can I help?"

She moved to the table and stroked Samson's fur. Harry was over at his counter working on his laptop. Close, but giving them space. "You're helping now. Just being here. Finding me."

Bryce's mesmerizing silvery-blue eyes held her gaze, and she didn't miss that they were filled with extraordinary pain.

"How can I ever thank you? If you hadn't come—"

"Then you don't… You don't blame me for using Samson to find you?"

Sierra took Bryce's hand. "How could I blame you for that? I tried to protect Samson the same way I tried to protect my heart. By avoiding the risks. I can't do that anymore. Samson saved us both today and I'll never forget that. He has to do what he was born and trained to do." She swallowed the tears welling in her throat. "Oh, Bryce, I was so afraid you were going to die. And for me. I had asked you to leave for a reason."

Her heart stuttered as she looked at him. She loved him. Yes, she loved him. She couldn't stop if she tried.

"But I didn't die." He took her other hand

in his. "I hope... I hope you'll change your mind about me leaving."

Tears flooded her cheeks. Okay. Not good. She swiped them away. "I can't stop myself from loving you, Bryce, no matter if I'm afraid to take the risk. Even if you leave, I'll still love you." She stepped closer until her face was a few inches from his. She looked up at him, remembering that kiss.

Emotion stirred behind his gaze. "I'm right here with you. We're together in this and we can always be together if you just... Just say the word. I won't leave." He let his gaze drop to Samson who breathed peacefully on the table. "And as long as Samson approves, of course."

Samson moaned and barked and rolled up to sit.

"Samson!" Sierra and Bryce shouted in unison.

"Oh, Samson." Sierra hugged his neck. Then she peered at his face. "You're okay. You're going to be okay."

Harry was at his side in a flash and listened to the dog's heart and breathing again. "The antidote worked. He sounds good all around. I think you can take your dog home, boys and girls."

Samson hopped from the table. Harry

poured water into a bowl and the dog lapped it up. Sierra crouched next to him, thrilled that he'd made it.

Samson licked her face, then Bryce's.

She laughed and then stood up. Bryce stood so close and she was drawn to him. She stepped into Bryce's arms. "I think Samson is giving his approval. His approval for... What did you mean when you said you wouldn't leave? Do you mean you're going to move out here to the middle of nowhere?"

He chuckled. "Only if that's okay with you."

"What are you really thinking?"

"I'm thinking I want to get a dog and have puppies with you and train them for SAR rescues. Anything to spend more time with you. I love you, Sierra. I thought my heart would stop when you said you loved me. What I'm really thinking... Okay, here it goes... I want to marry you. I've wanted that since the first year I knew you. What do you say?"

She stood on her toes and pressed her lips against his. Wrapped her arms around his neck and then up into his hair and pulled him closer to her, pouring all her answer into the kiss.

He broke away, leaving her breathless.

"Does that answer your question?"

\* \* \* \* \*

Dear Reader,

Thank you for reading *Fugitive Trail*! Some of you might recognize the scenery—the ice climbing park and festival—as what takes place in the small town of Ouray, Colorado. I changed the name and county so I didn't have to worry too much about the exact details but rather could have fun writing my story—you know, artistic license and all that! The toy store is loosely modeled after the real store there in Ouray—O'Toys, which is owned by my brother and sister-in-law! I had hoped to write a story that would include their store and the opportunity came when my editor contacted me about writing a story in Colorado. I love it when that happens!

I also love to hear from my readers. Please hop on over to my new website at elizabethgoddard.com to find ways to connect with me and sign up for my newsletter.

Blessings!
*Elizabeth Goddard*

# Get 4 FREE REWARDS!

## We'll send you 2 FREE Books plus 2 FREE Mystery Gifts.

**Harlequin Heartwarming Larger-Print** books will connect you to uplifting stories where the bonds of friendship, family and community unite.

FREE
Value Over
$20

# ReaderService.com has a new look!

We have refreshed our website and we want to share our new look with you. Head over to ReaderService.com and check it out!

**On ReaderService.com, you can:**

- Try 2 free books from any series
- Access risk-free special offers
- View your account history & manage payments
- Browse the latest Bonus Bucks catalog

**Don't miss out!**

If you want to stay up-to-date on the latest at the Reader Service and enjoy more Harlequin content, make sure you've signed up for our monthly News & Notes email newsletter. Sign up online at ReaderService.com.